Thrice a Bride

Michelle Janene

Thrice a Bride

Michelle Janene

STRONG TOWER
PRESS

Strong Tower Press, PO Box 293632, Sacramento, CA 95829
http://strongtowerpress.com

Cover Art by: Whetstone Designs
Images: Ocean - Unsplash Timo Voltz / stone wall - Unsplash Marc Pell / woman - Deposit photo id 504435636 Kislev Andrey
Dunnattor - Deposit Photo id
Fonts: Athelas; Medusa; Semplicita pro - Adobe
Interior Images: chapter divider - pixaby, Gordon Johnson - https://pixabay.com/vectors/divider-separator-line-art-5318234/
Birds - FreePNGlogos birds-g0b595d18d_1280.png
Sundial - public domain - https://openclipart.org/download/280075/Sundial_PSF.svg

ISBN: 978-1-942320-43-2

Chapter 1

He should never have begun this venture. It could end in doom for both of them. A rhythmic tap on his cabinet door raked Fergus' already raw nerves. "Aye." He punctuated the admittance with a groan.

His guard, Matthew, bowed and offered a slim smile. "She's arrived, m'laird."

Fergus pushed to his feet and straightened as much as his aged frame would allow. This endeavor was ill advised, but he'd taken pity on the lass. His man's smile grew as Fergus ambled to the door. His decision had made his kirth and kin happy, but still …

Nathair joined him in the passageway to the hall. "So, the little strumpet is at our gates." His son elbowed him. "Do ye still feel fruitful at yer age, Da? Lookin' for another heir to replace me?"

"Ye'll hold yer tongue, lad. I'll not have ye besmirching her fine character. The lass was in need, and I chose to aid her. Ye'll treat her with the respect due a lady of the manse."

They strolled into the hall side-by-side, but his son could not be more different from him. Wild, irreverent, sloven. Fergus sighed. Nothing he did produced any change in the lad. Nathair plopped onto the bench at the high table with an eager gaze on the door. A shiver danced over Fergus' skin and ended in a shudder. This venture was sore ill advised. Perchance bringing her here would do more harm. No, nothing could be more harmful than what her father intended for her.

The citizens of Seycoll gathered to glimpse their new lady. The eager mutters and amiable smiles betrayed their disfavor of Nathair ruling over them as their next laird. Yet again, Fergus regretted the deal he'd struck with the lass' father. But he had little time to bemoan his poor choices as Crom stomped into his hall and dragged the young lass beside him.

The lean man wore a perpetual scowl, drawing his face of wrinkles in long, harsh lines. He'd cropped his dark beard short, but flecks of food bits litter it. His plaid lay dirty and disheveled over his shoulders and flesh peeked through his trews.

The lass wore what looked to be new garments. A simple green overdress and cream chemise. The rich green set off her stunning, flame-red curly locks, which cascaded about her long oval face and over her shoulders. Her father didn't even allow her the kindness of brushing her hair before dumping her in the hall before a man of Fergus' standing.

"Have ye the papers to sign, Fergus?" The man released his unwanted charge.

Nathair snorted. "Is this the way all those outside our land greet the Fullarton laird?"

Crom, at least, had the common sense to look chastised and lowered into a quick bow. The lass curtsied slow and deep beside him.

Freed of her father's grasp, she rose, brushed hair from her face, and tried to contain its wild spirited strands behind her. Her long nose sat between pale cheeks sprinkled with freckles, as though the pixies had danced there and left prints. She looked touched by the mystical. Her gaze remained to the floor so Fergus couldn't see her eyes, but she clasped her hands gently before her. She didn't seem to tremble as she stood unmoving beside her sire.

"I thought we'd dine afore—"

Crom scowled, rolled his shoulders, and shifted his weight. "Pardon, m'laird, but I've business of import to be seein' to afore day's end. If we could be about the matter at hand, I'll leave ye to yer merry-makin'."

Fergus frowned, matching Crom's scowl with one of his own. Crom was a cruel man, well Fergus knew from dealing with him when Fergus had visited Ansmarkt. But the man made a point. They'd have a much more enjoyable afternoon after he left.

Fergus waved him to follow. "Come, all awaits in the cabinet." Matthew opened the door to his private study as the two men approached. Fergus had furnished his cabinet well with books and works of art. It sat adjacent to the hall. The contract concerning the lass lay on top of the small desk. The bag of coin remained hidden in a drawer.

Crom scanned it over. "Seems in order, but have ye the coin?"

Fergus shot a glance to his steward, Owen, who'd followed them inside. As Fergus suspected, Crom couldn't read. At least this one minor fact in this venture might work out for the best.

Selling a woman was distasteful, but Fergus had noted the men who had taken an interest in bargaining for Crom's lass. Fergus had feared for her safety and purity. He'd agreed to a larger sum than seemed fitting for a craftsman's daughter with a dubious claim to be from the lesser nobility. Still, Fergus had felt the need to protect her, but he'd put his own stipulations on Crom to produce her claim of noble lineage. Crom, for his part, insisted on a marriage between the young lass and the elder laird.

"Ye have what the laird requested?" Owen said with a nod to Fergus.

Crom pulled a folded parchment from his waist and offered it to whichever of them would take it.

Owen made a quick check of it. "There is the matter of her name, as well. I will need it to complete the contract before ye sign."

"Davina." The word near vomited out of Crom. "Of the Clan Moffat."

Owen added the name. Crom wouldn't take the quill to make his mark until he had the coins in hand. He shook the bag, opened it and pulled a handful out. Checking those left inside, he counted what remained in his hand as they dropped back in.

"Ye calling me a liar, Crom?" Fergus closed the distance between them. "I have standing with the traders in Ansmarkt to see none do business with ye again. And I may be old, man, but I can still knock ye on yer arse."

The coins clattered into the bag and he hid it away in the folds of his filthy plaid with the speed of a lightning strike. The quill scratched across the parchment.

Fergus added his signature to Crom's crude mark and the distasteful man bolted toward the door without being given leave. He stopped at the door just long enough to incline his head. "Good luck to ye."

Fergus followed the fleeing man. Crom passed Davina, who hadn't moved since they'd left. He slowed a fraction as he stormed past her toward the door. "I wash me hands of ye, girl. Ye kill this one too, and I'll not allow ye back."

Chapter 2

Her da's parting words hadn't been loud. Hopefully, none other than the laird had heard his hateful claim. It didn't matter. Crom was done with her. It was a good thing that Davina would never see him again.

The laird, her husband, stood beside her. She'd only glimpsed him before Crom had demanded to be free of her. She sighed. The man was once vigorous. It showed in the way he carried himself and the way the trews and tunic hung a little loose on him now. His shoulders slumped with age. His hair and beard were white and cut short.

"Lady Davina, do ye need some time to rest, or shall we dine first?"

By the saints, the man asked her what she wanted. She struggled to stifle the start racing through her body. There must be a correct answer. She pinched a bit of her lower lip between her teeth. Would he think she feared over her da's parting words if she sought to speak the rites? Perchance dining would allow him the freedom to reconsider his offer of marriage. What would she do if he changed his mind? With a contract signed between the laird and her sire, could the offer of marriage be broken?

"My lady?"

He may be testing her to see if she would seek her own way. "As it pleases m'laird." Did he sigh? Did she answer wrong? She steeled herself for the blow.

Laird Fergus' hand did raise, but it was to wave her toward the high table. "I think yer journey has been long and not as pleasant as it might have been with someone else. Let us eat."

She inclined her head to his kind words and waited to follow him. But when he again waved her forward, she took a tentative step toward the stairs. He followed at her elbow and they climbed onto the dais.

A younger man slouched at the table. Streaked with waves of brown and blond, his hair lay covered in a film of grime. She again fought to control her body's reactions, as his stench made her taste bile. His appraising glance swept from her head to her toes and back, causing her belly to twist into a knot.

Fergus waved her further along the table and, giving the other man a wide berth, took the place between them. "Seycoll, let us welcome Lady Davina to our hearth and home. May she bring joy and find joy all her days within these walls."

Davina had ceased taking her seat at the announcement, but when the entire hall exploded with cheers and rapped dirks on the tables, she plopped on her backside renewing the ache from the hasty ride clinging to Crom's shirt as she'd teetered behind his saddle. She bowed her head, tears pricked her eyes. What had the laird told them to make them so generous in their welcome of a humble tanner's daughter?

Her thoughts swung from incoherent to fretful, and she missed the prayer until a hearty "Amen" snatched her attention back to the joyful chatter. Food arrived from the kitchens and the laird filled her plate. By the saints, he offered her a heaping quantity. More than Crom allowed her in near three days.

"Welcome, my lady."

It would be poor manners to correct the man, for she was not of noble birth. She didn't ken to the tales Crom told. He was always a braggart. Better to just agree. She inclined her head.

"The day was fine for traveling." The authority and strength of his voice was kissed with gentleness.

Thank ye, Lord. It had been her consistent prayer that no matter what Crom intended for her, God would bring her to a place of peace.

The smelly man at the end of the table leaned toward them. "Well, at least she'll not pester ye with nigglin' chatter, Father. Let's hope she serves ye're other purpose more amenably."

"Nathair." A growl rumbled from the elder man at his petulant son and rose the hairs on Davina's neck and arms. "Shut ye're mouth or be gone with ye."

Nathair slid to the end of the bench and winked. Davina fought a shudder.

"Forgive me son, lass. I did right in raisin' him, swear I did, but …" The laird sighed, sagging his shoulders further.

She again offered him an incline of her head. They ate in silence and Davina left almost half on her plate. Would the laird think ill of her? Think her wasteful?

She couldn't help it. She couldn't eat another bite without retching.

"Shall we retire to the solar for the afternoon?" He didn't sound displeased.

She rose, and he offered his arm. The saints help her. He welcomed her touch. No one ever touched her—except in punishment. Davina fought to calm her rattled thoughts. There was a proper way to take his arm. She'd seen a noble couple do it once. Did she wrap her arm around his, or place it on top? Oh, this was not going well.

Chapter 3

Again, the lass chewed on a bit of her lip. Was she afraid?
Perchance she didn't favor what she believed was a marriage to one who
could be her grandsire. At last, her hand alighted over his with a touch
of a butterfly. Fergus smiled, and she released a breath. Fergus
misunderstood. The poor lass had not feared him, but she'd been unsure
of what to do with his offered hand.

Fergus swallowed an angry growl and led them from the hall into the
keep. Whether she had any noble blood or nay, Crom had done nothing
to see to the lass' simple education. Was she a simpleton or did neglected
and mistreated keep her silent? The next days would be interesting.

Unfortunately, before they could exit the hall, his people rose and
lined a path from the dais steps to the outer door. Fie. They expected
consents to be exchanged and blessings given. His kirth and ken clapped
their approval and encouragement, and there was now no other option
but to go where they led. This was not going as he'd hoped.

Stepping from the hall, the perpetual coastal winds caught at
Davina's unbound hair and whipped it about her face. Some of the long
tresses even caught at his eyes in their wild snaking about.

Her head rose but a little, and her gaze wandered over her current home. Seycoll was a high round bluff barely attached to the coastline by a bit of sand spanning the bottom of a deep gorge. They could defend their near-island with ease due to the sheer cliffs leading up to tall walls. Did Davina favor it as he did?

Without removing her left hand from his, she snatched as much hair as she could contain with her right and held it in a fearsome grip at the nape of her neck. He thought he heard a soft growl of frustration, but otherwise she seemed quite calm.

His kirth and kin lined the small path all the way to the kirk, singing and cheering as the couple passed. Davina's cheeks pinked, and she lowered her head again.

They stopped at the steps of the holy building. He would not lead them inside and would not involve the priest. This would have to be enough to appease his people. Fergus took both her hands. "Lady Davina, I take ye."

She paused only a moment to look at where his hand held hers. "Laird Fergus, I take ye to be me husband."

The good people erupted in cheers, and she startled again. She staggered back a step hand he lost his connection to her. His kin's boisterous singing brought them back to the hall, where the floor sat clear of the tables and music filled every corner. Fergus hoped to sit in the solar and get acquainted and inform her of the state of their union, but his people clapped in rhythm, waiting for them to begin.

"Shall we dance, Davina?"

She inclined her head, ran her fingers through her hair, twisting it into a long cord, and looped it into a loose knot before she followed him to the center of the room.

She stood, facing her husband. What an odd thing. Husband. This man had to be over sixty summers, perchance even seventy. But his grasp of her hands in front of the kirk had been firm and yet gentle. The foreign sensation of another holding her—skin against skin—left a tingle behind and a gnawing ache in her heart to be touched again.

Davina held her breath and prayed they would do a dance she'd watched before. She'd never joined in; never allowed to take part. But she'd watched many from the shadows and tried them alone in the dark after Crom was long in bed.

They raised their hands as the music struck the notes of the reel. *Thank You, Lord.* She clapped both palms with Fergus three times, followed by three more times with their left hands and another three with their right. Linking elbows, they twirled one direction, before switching to the other arm and spinning the other direction. Bouncing in step from their heels to their toes, they did the traditional steps and began again.

Fergus kept pace with her and didn't seem the least bit winded as he twirled her to a man of his clan. Men and women formed concentric rings, men on the inner and women on the outer. She completed each clap, twirl, and swing around the ring of men before she returned to the laird again. Still, he seemed spry and when the music changed and they formed lines of the next reel. It was less familiar to her, but he led her through the steps.

Laughter filled the room and Davina breathed a little deeper. Smiles and gentle hands greeted her at every turn, blurring together in a pool of touch and joy. Something about this place washed away the days filled with anxious prayers of what would await her at the end of her journey. Crom did well by her, though she was sure it hadn't been his intent.

She twirled free of one man to be caught by the laird's elbow and spun around. His laughter was boisterous. No, Crom never cared where she went or what would happen to her. This man, Laird Fullarton, assured she was brought here and did not allow her to be sentenced to some hell. She would have to find a way to show her gratitude.

An elbow gripped hard in her next exchange, pinching her. She needn't look up at this man, for his stench told her Nathair danced beside her now. After so many circuits, it was hard to hold her breath, but she tried.

"Ye're a right bonny lass. If ye ever tire of the bed of a shriveled ancient man …"

Chapter 4

After some eight or nine dances, Fergus' age wore on him. But he hated to pull Davina from the revelry. Though he had yet to see her eyes as she kept her head low, she did smile. Shy, but genuine, it told him he'd done right by her. His people were already growing fond of her and she would find a place in their hearts quickly. He hoped it would be a good thing in the end. She slipped into his heart as he watched her loop and whirl around the hall. He knew what it would cost him, but he couldn't help it.

Nathair partnered with her. She stiffened, shied away, and disentangled from him in haste. A few men later, she joined arms with Fergus again. This time, when the music started again, she hesitated. Looking about the dancers, she stopped when her glance landed on Nathair and she turned to leave the floor.

"Ye are tired?"

Her lip disappeared between her teeth again, and her head sank low. Fergus put out his arm. "Shall we now retire to the solar?"

They slipped from the hall with few noticing, or at least none drew attention. Winding up the staircase to the third floor, he nudged open the double carved doors and allowed her to step into the bright space.

This was his favorite room. The late afternoon sun glowed through the three large windows, bathing the comfortable chairs and couches in warmth. The fire had been lit, and he added a bit of wood to it before turning to sit.

Davina hadn't moved from the place where he left her inside the door. Hands again clasped before her, head bowed, she wouldn't move without direction.

He paused before her, cupped her cheek in his hand, and raised her face until their gazes met. By the sword, if she didn't have the most bewitching eyes. The palest blue, like ice on a stream, with black centers so small they almost disappeared within the pale orbs. Her gaze said a thousand things. The loudest of them fear, for Crom raised her under his cruel hand, and she expected like treatment here.

Fergus lost himself in her fright. Oh, how he wished he could wipe her memory of every terrible day before this one. "'Tis a blessing to have ye here, lass."

Her narrow brows drew together and her head tipped, leaning more into his hand.

"I can nay imagine growing up under the harsh hand of that foul man who claimed to be yer sire, but things will be different here. None will ever raise a hand to ye. And never will a harsh word be used to cut ye low."

A slim smile graced her face, and tears pooled in those enchanting eyes. "Thank ye, m'laird."

A tear slid free and Fergus brushed it away. "Ye are lady of the manse. Ye must call me Fergus." He stepped away and lowered his hand to her elbow.

She flinched at his gentle touch.

"Are ye hurt?" He took her wrist when she didn't answer and pushed up her sleeve. Several small oval bruises encased her slender arm. "I should see that man flogged. I'll never darken his shop again. Others will follow. He'll pay, lass, for every evil thin' he did to ye." He directed her to sit in a chair beside a small table. "And ye are never to wait for permission to sit anywhere ye choose, or go about to any place within our walls. This be yer home."

She slid down to a cushioned seat and lowered her head. "I don't ken how to thank ye."

"Hold yer head up high and be the proud lady of Seycoll while yer here."

"Pride goeth before a fall." It was such a quiet whisper that he wasn't sure she'd said it.

"I'm sure Crom beat those words into ye, lass, but does not the holy book also say, 'I will praise thee, for I am fearfully and wondrously made: marvelous are thy works, and my soul knoweth it well?'"

Her head came up and a dying ray of sunlight danced in her eyes. "Thank ye, my—Fergus." Her voice had the quality of the fairy folk. Like a gentle breeze that could be missed if one didn't pay heed.

"Is there a drink ye favor?"

Her gaze fluttered and, again, she hesitated.

"There is no wrong answer, Davina. Ye're entitled to yer own opinions."

"I've only had water and weak wine."

Fergus pulled an earthenware jug from the shelf and filled a cup. He handed it to her with a smile.

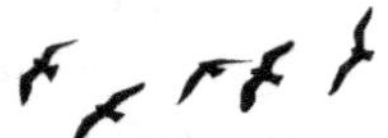

Davina sipped at the near black liquid with some trepidation. A sweet, heady flavor kissed by summer berries danced over her tongue and warmed her. She tasted it again, more deeply.

The door burst open, and she nearly slouched the remaining contents over her new gown.

Nathair strolled into the room. "Father, *Mother*." He winked at her, and she lowered her gaze. The man made her skin crawl.

"What are ye doin'?" Fergus grumbled at his son.

She considered Laird Fergus Fullarton as he squared off with the man who was perchance five years her senior. Fergus had asked her to call him by his Christian name as her da had done. But while Crom did it so none would mark her as his daughter, Fergus made the request as a sign of her position and the intimacy that was to be between them. She marveled at how the same request could produce such contrary emotion within her.

Nathair strolled between them. "This is the *family* solar. And are we not still family? Ye haven't replaced me yet?" He stood beside her and glanced into her cup. "Needing to ply the lass with drink before ye bed her? I recommend something stronger than mead—"

In two quick strides, Fergus closed the distance to his son and punched him.

Chapter 5

Rocked back on his feet, Nathair staggered a step away from his father's assault and rubbed his unruly beard.

"Get out!" Fergus' words were a menacing growl so similar to what Davina had heard from Crom on far too many occasions. Fergus was nay the weak old man she'd thought him. His warrior's heart still beat within. She stifled a shudder and admonished herself to always remember he could be fierce as well as gentle.

But Fergus' tender hand came to rest on her shoulder. "Davina is now the lady of the manse and ye shall treat her with the honor due her and me as yer father. If ye can nay abide such, find yer way elsewhere."

Nathair opened his mouth, but Fergus released her and closed his fist again. The younger man left, slamming the door.

Davina broke the silence staling the air between them. "I'm sorry for troubling yer home, Fergus."

"Never apologize for him again." His words were harsh and made her flinch. He softened as he took the chair beside her and her hand.

The sensation of having her hand held again filled her until she almost missed what Fergus was saying.

"There was trouble in me home long before ye arrived, lass. 'Tis nay to do with ye." His grip tightened, and he captured her gaze. "Promise me, Davina, ye'll stir well clear of Nathair. I fear what he may …" Fergus shook his head. "Don't get caught alone with him and don't let him harm ye. No matter what it takes, defend yerself."

While she reveled at being touched, her stomach churned. She nodded as she pressed her arm against the ache in her middle.

"Say it, lass. Swear to me ye'll be on guard where that blighter is concerned."

"I vow to watch, be alert, and pray." She squeezed his hand, hoping he'd never let go, but he slumped back into his chair and her hand slipped out of his. He didn't speak for some time as he rubbed at his temples. Should she have done that for him? Would he welcome her touch when Crom had despised it? "Might we speak forthright, Davina?"

"Aye."

"The lad was born late in me marriage. Sile, me wife, was so overjoyed at being a mum at last, she favored the boy over much. We

now pay for her overindulgence. Sile was a powerful, willful woman. Now I can nay rein in his ill behavior. He is me heir and the only I shall ever have." He looked at her again. Did he say what she thought?

"Aye, lass. Ye'll be lady of the manse only. I'm too old to do more for ye. I'm sorry, but I had to agree to Crom's bargain."

So she would be an untouched bride. At least Fergus was kind. It seemed the best she could have hoped for. She stared at the dancing flames and sipped of her mead. "Why did ye?"

"He bartered his own blood to any depraved creature who had coin. I saw the men who sought to own ye." He shook his head. "Would have been a hell I'd nay wish on any woman. I knew I couldn't be a proper husband and Nathair could be a danger, but better this than what yer da had planned, lass."

He'd seen Crom's intentions with clarity. "Thank ye again, Fergus."

He leaned forward, forearms resting on his knees. "What'd ye do to make Crom so bent on punishing ye?"

Davina shrugged and sipped at the mead again. She rather liked this drink. "I was born a lass and hale."

Fergus' brow rose. "He has sons less than hale, then?"

"Crom lost three afore they were five summers. None from me mum. She said it were God's punishment for all his evil adulterin' ways." Davina twisted the cup in her hand as she stared at the last of its contents.

"Ye're nay a punishment, Davina."

"Aye, God has a purpose. He promises a hope and future." She lifted her cup to him. "I think it may start here."

Fergus offered her a slim smile in return to her toast. "Didn't yer mum try to stop him?"

"I imagine she did, but Ma died while I did life-cycle service. When I returned to Crom, he sought other ways to be rid of me."

Fergus leaned back, elbows on the arms of his chair, and steepled his fingers. "What service did ye learn?"

"Spinning and weaving."

He sighed as his head hung low. "And yer first husband?"

"I was married an hour. We exchanged our consents before Mr. Ealar's kin and he went to his chamber. A servant found him dead on his floor. I saw him for all of a handful of minutes as we spoke the rites. I can nay figure how I killed him, but Crom swore."

"Crom is a fool. Ye did naught. Think no more on the matter."

She nodded. She'd never blamed herself. "If I'm not to … If we're never …" She took a deep breath. "What do ye require of me, Fergus?"

"Ye are the lady of the manse. Ye'll oversee the running of the affairs within and those who serve."

Davina covered her mouth to keep from spitting the last of her mead all over him. Oh, saints help her.

Chapter 6

Fergus slipped into bed early. Weariness pulled at his old bones. The celebration still continued in the hall below and he'd told Davina she could rejoin them. She'd chosen to go to her chamber as well, however.

She'd surprised him. Never bemoaned her state of being what she would no doubt consider an untouched bride. But if Fergus could complete his plan … He sighed as he pulled the covers over him to ward off the chill coming from both his room and his heart.

No, Davina was a rare woman. From Nathair's crude intrusion to Fergus' many questions, little had provoked a reaction from her. Though she'd nearly choked when he'd told her she'd run the household. Crom had left her ill prepared for this new life. Correcting that would be his first order of business. And the next would be to set the rest to right as well.

"M'lady, what—"

Davina jumped as a common-dressed woman entered her chamber before the sun peaked through the shutters. "The Laird said my duties were to oversee certain matters. I thought it best to get an early start."

"Saints alive, m'lady, only the baker is up at this hour, she is." She snatched Davina's gown from her arms before she could pull it over her head and twisted it around her arm. "Nay. 'Tis nay fine enough for the lady wife of the laird. Nay fine enough at all."

"But 'tis new." The only new thing Crom had ever given her. She reached for it.

The woman crinkled her nose and returned the simple gown. They met eye to eye. The woman were blue too, but darker like the sea outside crashing against the cliffs. What a wondrous sound. The woman shook her round head. "Well, 'tis nay fine enough for our lady. Just 'tsn't." Her plain kirtle swished around her full-figure as she opened the tall wardrobe against the wall near the door. An array of fine wool and linen gowns and other things hung within. "For yer first day …" Short stocky fingers ran over several, as the woman glanced over her shoulder and back at the dresses. "Nay red. Blue?" She drew a deep blue dress out and held it. "Aye! Blue is most fittin'. It is." She closed the cabinet and waved Davina to follow through the door to a washroom. "Now, off with that." She pointed to the chemise Davina had slept in. "I'll help ye wash and dress. I will."

Davina clutched the thin cloth against her skin. "My lad—mam … I … But …"

"Izbeil, m'lady." She stepped toward Davina. "Izbeil," she repeated. "Now, off with that and we'll get ye cleaned and dressed. We will."

Davina sputtered and inched toward the door. "Izbeil, I can …"

Izbeil's hands propped on her wide hips. "The laird says I am to be yer personal maid. I am. I'll nay have him cross with me 'causin' yer a shy lass. Come now."

Maid. Well, of course the lady of the manse would have people attend her. She quaked as Izbeil seized her chemise and whisked it over her head.

Izbiel's mouth opened wide. "Ye've nary any undergarments."

Davina swallowed her shame as it warmed her skin. The woman, who carried more weight and less shape than Davina's neglected frame, vanished from the room. Drawers and cupboards opened and banged closed. Izbeil soon returned with an armful of unbleached cloth items. Once her maid had collected all the desired items and set aside, Izbeil proceed to wash her with water kissed by a harebell scent.

No one had bathed her since she was a wee child. Heat filled more than her cheeks before Izbeil was satisfaction. "We'll get ye a proper bath this eve. We will. We ain't 'ad a proper lady livin' in the manse for too long now. Too long. But I'll see a tub brought in. I will."

Dressed in layer upon layer, Izbeil moved Davina to the small chair near the fire and set about arranging her hair in torturous rows of braids she swirled into all manner of designs. She blinked away the tears as Izbeil surveyed her work. "*Now*, ye can meet with the laird and break yer fast. Ye can." She opened the chamber door and then the doors to the solar across the hall.

Davina looked at the unmade bed and to her discarded clothes strewn about.

"I'll put everythin' ta right, m'lady. I will."

"Please don't get rid of the green dress," she whispered.

Izbeil sighed. "As ye wish."

Her slippers sat lost under the billowing fabric, and she tripped several times before plopping in a seat. She fidgeted. Davina had no idea what overseeing the running of a household would entail, but surely, she should have been trying to learn it and not sitting here. She tried to stand, stepped on her hem, and crashed. Climbing to her seat again, she cleared the fabric and stood.

"Good morrow." Fergus stood in the doorway, dressed in trews and a long-belted tunic. She smoothed her gown. She'd match him better in her own dress.

"Good morrow."

"Ye're up early."

"There is work to do—"

"Not this day, lass." He put his arm out and she inched toward him, as she tried not to stumble. "After we eat, I'll show ye the manse and introduce ye to the people."

Several times during the meal, Davina winced and touched at her braids. Fergus asked, but she wouldn't speak.

"Davina, 'tis clear ye're in pain."

"'Tis nothing."

He took her hand before she could fill her spoon with porridge again. "Ye must tell me what troubles ye. 'Tis me duty."

"Izbeil meant only for me to make a good impression." She fidgeted with the braids again.

Fergus saw the maid cross the hall. "Izbeil, come."

"Please don't scold her."

Izbeil curtsied.

"Nay, I shant admonish a maid when her mistress will nay speak her need."

"Ye have need, m'lady?" Izbeil crumbled her apron in her hands.

"Fie, woman." He huffed as Davina cowered beside him. "Iz, the coif ye made causes pain."

The maid gasped, genuflected multiple times, and muttered her apologies.

"Cease yer fussin', Iz. The lady should have spoken." He waved them off, and they disappeared.

CHAPTER 7

When Davina returned to Fergus, the throbbing in her skull was dissipating. She'd convinced Izbeil to just plait it in one simple, loose strand for the remainder of the day. She draped the end over her shoulder to keep it from continuing to irritate her tender scalp.

Fergus offered his arm with a smile and led her from the hall. Gray clouds hid the walls, but not the sound of the salt-tinted waves crashing far below. She wanted to get another glimpse of the rugged coastline she'd noticed when she arrived. Wind whistled past her ears. At least her hair was bound this time and she could see everything not hidden by the fog. From the gate, the road disappeared out of sight, only to climb up the other side to come even with where they stood now.

As she came to the bottom step of the keep, she hesitated. Fergus' boots sunk into the mud left by an early morning shower.

"Davina?"

"I don't wish to muddy these lovely skirts."

"Mud washes."

"But the work."

"'Tis why ye have maids." He laced their fingers together and gave her a gentle pull. Dampness invaded her slippers and squished between her toes in a matter of steps.

Buildings nestled against the tall walls left a large open space for the laird's people to gather. Connected to the kirk was the storehouse, where a young squire organized new items. The smithy's hammer tapped out a welcoming rhythm. And the garron ponies tossed their heads with soft whinnies of greeting. A breeze eased over the wall, kissed with salt from the sea, and whispered *'home'*.

Tears pricked at her eyes as it whispered again *'home'*. It was all she ever wanted, a place to belong. Could it be here?

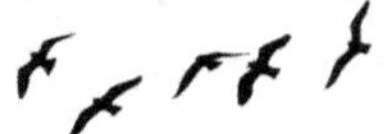

As they passed the falcons, Davina paused and closed her eyes.

"Is something amiss, lass?"

She shook her head but didn't move.

"Lass?" She'd stopped. Was she ill? Did something about his home displease her?

Her head shook again. "I'm trying to remember."

"What?"

"The squire organizing the stores is Will. Robert, the smithy, is married to Molly, the cook. Duncan, the groom, is wed to Izbeil and is assisted by three lads …"

Fergus staggered as Davina listed every person they had met this morn to the man—by name. She even knew their kin. "By the sword. Ye've learned near two score of those who live in the manse in less than an hour, lass."

Her ice-blue eyes opened and looked at him. Her head tipped. "Is this not what I am to do? As lady of the manse, are these not now my kin? Is it not our responsibility to care for them and assure their welfare along with our own?"

Fergus patted her hand as they resumed walking. "True enough, but ye need not learn them all in a single morn. I would nay have believed a thing even possible."

After finishing half the circuit around the manse, again, Davina paused. She looked up at the high wall. "Might we …?" Her head lowered, and she continued the way they had been walking.

"Would ye fancy to stand atop the wall?"

She nipped at her lip again. "If we might?" It was a question more than a request.

He led her to the stairs nestled against the wall. "Ye are the lady. Ye may go anywhere that pleases ye."

Facing the North Sea, her eyes closed, and her shoulders relaxed. A slim smile graced her thin lips.

Fergus couldn't take his eyes off her. Had he only been a few score younger. "Ye like our little near-isle."

"Oh, aye. 'Tis …"

"Home?"

She only nodded, but her smile grew.

"'Tis rare to find one nay born to Seycoll who loves it as we." He let the wind and the sea bid greeting, as it snatched strands of fire from her plait. After a time, her eyes opened and her gaze swept the length of the coast, before she turned and looked down into the manse.

"Thank ye, Fergus." His raised brow caused her to continue. "For allowing me to come."

"'Tis me great joy." Would she still thank him when the rest of his plan was complete? He offered his arm, and they continued. Davina persisted in devoting each name to memory. "Shall we go to midday meal?"

She glanced toward the sun, now visible through the last wisps of fog. "Heavens, is it time to eat again?"

Fergus laughed and patted her hand as they made their way back to the hall.

Chapter 8

Davina spent the afternoon meeting the household staff. Her head ached, but she thought she remembered everyone's name. Tomorrow would be the test. She retired to her room with the setting sun.

"Are ye ready for a bath, m'lady?" Izbeil entered on her heels.

Tell her what ye need. No need to get her in Fergus' cross sights again. "If I can get a basin to wash my feet, I'd like to take me bath in the morn."

"Of course, m'lady."

Davina warmed herself by the fire as the maid bustled about around her. "Izbeil, may I have some buttons, several lengths of ribbon, a needle, and thread?"

Izbeil busied herself drawing garments out of drawers and turning down the bed. "The seamstress can see to yer needs. She can. What do ye require?"

"I don't wish to trouble Fiona. I just need these few items."

The motherly maid stopped and looked at Davina with her fists on her hips. "But, m'lady—"

Davina walked to the window and looked out across the southern coast. "Izbeil, am I the lady of the manse?"

"Aye, that's right true."

Drawing in a deep breath to shore up her courage, she continued, though her voice was only a breath above a whisper. "Laird Fergus says I may do as I please and go where I please. Is this true?"

Izbeil was curt with her answer. "Aye, m'lady. True enough."

She glanced at the maid again. She was probably a score of years older than Davina, who was two-score and two. Yet the woman seemed to want to treat her like a child in need of … Well, she wasn't sure what Izbeil hoped. "Might I have buttons, ribbon, a needle, and thread?"

Izbeil curtsied. "Of course, m'lady." She slipped from the room.

Well, her first instructions caused Davina to wince as her lungs constricted and her heart struggled to beat. She didn't want to be harsh and demanding like her father. But Fergus expected her to command the staff. Maybe not command, but direct? What was the difference? How was she to lead if even her personal maid wouldn't do as she requested?

She released the air trapped in her aching lungs as she plopped down onto the stool near the fire. She wiggled out of her sodden slippers and warmed her numb toes by the flames, as she loosed her plait and worked on the many hard to reach ties of her gown.

"Have I displeased ye, m'lady?"

Davina brushed away a tear and lowered her head. "Nay, Izbeil. Forgive me."

Izbeil knelt, setting the basin of water she carried at Davina's feet. "Come now, m'lady. There be no need for such distress. No need at all."

"There is great need, for I've no idea how to be the lady of the manse." How much should she tell the maid? Could she trust her not to inform the entire keep of her insecurities?

"Yer feet are like ice. They are."

"The keep was quite soggy this morn as the laird showed me my new home."

Izbeil held Davina's foot and poured warm water over it into a basin. "Ye need proper boots. Ye do. Yer da was a tanner, was he not?"

"Aye, but he'd not waste his precious leather on me." Her words were more bitter than normal.

Izbeil was kind enough not to comment on her father. "Well, the laird is a kind man. He is. And he'll give ye what ye need. He will."

Her feet clean and warm, Izbeil helped her out of the many layers, and into a night trail. "I'll take these to be laundered. Do ye require anythin' more, m'lady?"

"Nay, Izbeil. Thank ye."

Izbeil paused at the door and put a small jingling bag on the table. "The items ye requested. And if it isn't out of place to be sayin' so, m'lady, ye're too hard on yerself. Yer are. Been here less than a day and already worryin' about performing yer duties perfect like. 'Tis too much, I say. The manse has managed without any direction from a lady for many years, right fine. If ye watch and learn before makin' people do as ye think best, they'll be more willin' to obey ye. They will."

"Thank ye, Izbeil."

The maid bent a knee before she took removed the soiled garments.

Davina collected the bag of sewing items and one gown from the wardrobe. Sitting on her huge over-stuffed bed with a mountain of pillows behind her, she attached loops of ribbon at intervals on the hem and buttons about a hand's length above them to the underside of the skirt. Never again would she soil these fine gowns with three inches of mud for someone else to spend hours removing.

She finished one dress, replaced it in the wardrobe, and began another. The candles burned low before her gaze blurred and she couldn't stop yawning. Five gowns hung ready for the soggy yard. Only three times as many remained. Heavens, a lady had a lot of dresses.

She secured the little of her remaining supplies and slipped under the covers. Bright rays of moonlight streamed through the glass beyond the open shutters and crashing waves lulled her to sleep too quickly. *Thank ye, Lord, for bringing me to Seycoll. May I never leave until I join Ye.*

Chapter 9

Davina stood at her window, watching the sun kiss the fog with light, when Izbeil knocked. The maid handed her a plaid to cover her sheer nightwear as a troop of older lads flowed through her chamber, carrying buckets full of steaming water. They carried each to the large metal tub that now stood in her bathing chamber.

She thanked each by name, which caused stumbled steps and curious stares. When they finished and left, Izbeil ushered her toward the waiting bath. "Why were they so startled?" she asked as Izbeil again stripped her. Wishing to hide, she stepped into the searing water and gasped. She added her other foot with more care and eased herself down.

"I don't think the Lady S"le ever bothered to learn anyone's name. I don't. And ye seem to know each of us in a day. 'Tis a wonder. It is." Izbeil wet a cloth and washed her.

Several moments passed and Davina remained silent. Izbeil paused. "Ye don't favor the bath?"

"'Tis quite wonderful," Davina said and nibbled on her lip.

Izbeil tsked and shook her head. "Again, ye ain't sayin' the full truth, m'lady. Forgive me for sayin' so."

With a sigh, Davina spoke what was on her mind. This place was so foreign for others to care what she thought on a matter. "'Tis so much work for so many. They must have far more important tasks than indulging me in a luxury that could as easily be taken care of with a damp cloth as we did yesterday. I have managed with the like quite fine for a score of years."

Izbeil paused in her scrubbing and looked at Davina with a raised brow and a small twist of her lips. "Were ye lady of the manse, then?"

"Nay." Davina slipped under the water with a groan and rinsed the soap from her hair.

"Well, ye are now. 'Tis our duty to tend our laird and lady well. We take pride in a providin' for ye. We do."

Davina hadn't thought of it in that manner. She would have to pray about it before upsetting the entire keep with her refusal.

Izbeil moved to the outer chamber.

"Please choose a gown from the five on the right."

Izbeil returned with a deep green one and helped Davina dry and dress. Izbeil brushed her hair dry near the fire before plaiting it. Careful not to pull too tight, she worked in two braids on either side of her head. She secured the ends near where they began, so they formed a loop beside her ears.

It felt odd, but not painful. What was wrong with a simple plait down the back? Everything seemed to be a fuss. Baths, multiple-layered garments, complicated hairstyles, heaps of food. It was all too much for a simple neglected tanner's daughter.

Izbeil opened the bedchamber door and moved the few steps across the hall to the solar.

Davina followed her out of her room, but didn't continue into the family room. "I wish to visit the kirk before the meal. I shall meet the laird at boards."

"As ye wish, m'lady."

While Izbeil returned to Davina's room to straighten and see to the damp towels, Davina wound down the narrow stairs. The smell hit her before she saw him. Between the second floor, where his room lay, and the bottom, Nathair staggered up toward her.

Davina stopped, one foot planted on a step and the other dangling above the one below. Should she go up to the second-floor landing to give him room? Would he just pass her in the tight space?

Don't get caught alone with him, and don't let him harm ye. Fergus' words rattled within her.

Nathair glimpsed her, and his head rose. His gaze raked over her. A menacing smile parted his lips.

If she ran from him now, she'd forever be doing so. She stepped down one more stair, though she remained out of his reach. She moved to descend another. *Please, Lord, make him let me pass.*

Nathair's palms pressed against both walls, barring her way. "Fleeing Father's bed before the sun?"

"Ye'll not talk to me so, sir. My affairs are none of yer concern."

He stepped up, his gaze again running the length of her. Vapors of fermented drink washed over her. Did the man drink it or bathe in it? "They could be."

"Nathair, make way. I have matters to attend."

Another step up. Good heavens, the man reeked. She blinked back tears.

"And what will ye give me for passage, lass?" When he moved one arm to reach out to her, he swayed.

Davina darted forward, ducked under his arm still braced against the wall, and hastened down the remaining stairs. Within a matter of steps, she careened around the last curve, skirts in hand.

Matthew, Fergus' personal guard, appeared in her path at the bottom. He jumped and his hands flew out to catch her before she slammed into him. "M'lady?" He glanced behind her. "Is all ta right?"

She released her skirts, caught her breath, and nodded. "Thank ye,

Matthew." She moved toward the hall and he fell into step behind her.

"What caused ye to descend the stairs in such a reckless manner? Ye could have been hurt." His kind words were heaped with genuine concern.

She continued on her way, but Matthew stepped in her path. Two men had blocked her way in a matter of minutes. This man didn't make her skin crawl, however. Arms crossed, stance wide, this man was a more imposing figure than a slobbering foul mouth. Matthew wore a clean tunic and trews, and a weapon hung at his hip. A good couple of stones larger than Nathair, but Matthew kept himself well groomed. He did not leer but looked at her as a brother would a beloved sister. The concern drew Matthew's brows together, and the soft hint of a smile banished any fears.

"I encountered Nathair on the stairs."

The man grew taller, shoulders squared. "Did he harm ye, m'lady?"

"Nay, unless ye account for his stench."

Matthew laughed, turning heads of the few who were beginning their day. He quieted and looked at her with a hard stare. "Are you tellin' me true, m'lady? Nathair did naught to hurt ye?"

She rubbed a chill away. "Nay, his only affront was curd words. I thank ye for yer concern and for saving me from a nasty tumble. If I might continue to the kirk?"

Matthew stepped out of her path, but his echoing steps continued to follow her.

The fog hung low, giving a nip to the air. Puddles, though smaller than yesterday, littered the ground. Before descending the steps, Davina bent and hooked the loops she'd added to her hem over the buttons.

"Hmmm."

Davina didn't look at Matthew behind her. "I know all can see me ankles, sir, but I'll not add to Blair and Cait's labors to clean the mud out." She marched down three steps and tried to traverse the driest route.

"I'm thinkin' yer right clever, m'lady. And thoughtful besides. Give it a few days, a sennight at most, and every lass in the manse will be doin' likewise."

Oh, saints above, what would Fergus think of all the women in his home flaunting their ankles with brazen disregard for their modesty? She failed to see a deep puddle as she fretted over her husband's view of her corrupting the entire manse. She sank near to her raised hem, and the sudden drop pitched her off balance.

Matthew caught her flailing arm, his other hand landing on the small of her back. "Careful, m'lady. 'Twould be a shame to save the hem, only to coat the rest in mud."

Davina righted herself, but the mud kept her slipper when she stepped free. She bit down on a growl.

Matthew laughed and handed her the sodden bit of fabric. "Ye need boots."

"I hope to ask the laird today."

"He'd not be refusin' ye, m'lady." He held open the kirk door.

She left her slippers on the stoop and padded in her bare feet to the altar. The door closed, but he hadn't followed. Kneeling on the bottom step, she bowed her head and thanked God for all the joy flooding her heart.

Chapter 10

"Oh, ye gave me a start."

Davina glanced up from her prayers to see Brother Patrick holding his hand to his chest. He stood at the end of the altar, with an open door to his living quarters behind him. "Forgive me, Brother Patrick."

"Are ye ta right, sister?"

She couldn't suppress her smile. "Oh, aye. I came to thank the Lord for all He's done for me. I also find my day progresses less disastrously when I begin it by meeting with Him."

The brother's shoulders relaxed and his arms hung at his side. He looked little like a holy man. Replace his long black tunic with a short one and trews, and put a sword in his hand and he could have stood beside Matthew, Robert, and the others in defense of their home. Home —she still stumbled at that word.

"Ye are welcome here anytime. The Lord is happy to hear His people." He strolled toward her and, before she could stand, his massive hand covered the crown of her head. Warmth from his sudden touch filled her. "The Lord bless ye and keep ye. The Lord make His face to shine upon ye and give ye peace."

"Amen." The word slipped out in a sigh. How she loved hearing

God's word. Tears pooled.

"Lady Davina?"

She shook her head and swiped at an escaping drop. "I don't recall anyone ever wishing me blessed. I'm ever grateful God has given me a place here."

Patrick straightened and clasped his hands in front of him. "Well, if I've heard true, 'tis us who're more blessed by ye, sister."

"Thank ye, Brother Patrick." She staggered to her feet in the many layers around her legs.

"Sister! Where are yer shoes?" Patrick's hand again went to his chest.

She lowered her head. "Being a holy place, and having rather soiled slippers, I thought of Moses and removed them before I came near the Lord."

Patrick threw back his head and laughed. The roar filled the room. He stroked his beard with a small shake of his head. "I'll be needin' to hone me messages with such a devoted sister in our congregation." He bowed. "As I said, your presence blesses us."

Matthew waited outside for her. Her toes curled at the chilled dampness as she slipped into her shoes again. She turned back toward the keep but Matthew waved her the other direction. "Let's see about those boots now."

"But I haven't—"

"To tell ye the truth, m'lady, Laird Fergus would tan me hide if I left ye to suffer when Quinn is right here."

She considered him for a long moment.

Matthew waved her forward. "I'll take the blame if it comes to that."

"I couldn't—" Davina shook her head.

He raised both hands in surrender. The slim smile almost hidden by his dark beard. "Please, m'lady."

She remembered Izbeil's words and inclined her head. She followed him out the gate to a small bit of land with a hut hugging the wall. With the help of Quinn's daughter, the tanner collected her measurements, and the tanner promised to have her boots finished within a few days.

By the time they re-entered the gate, the early morning sun was breaking through the fog. She went to the wall and climbed the stairs to stand where she had with Fergus that first time. Five rays broke through the gray sky like the hand of God reaching down to touch the shimmering sea. Gulls cried. Waves crashed. Wind rustled. The breath in her lungs eased out to join the wind and her eyes closed. *Saints, there is such peace here.* She allowed herself a moment more of bliss before descending the stairs to see to the work of the day ahead.

Matthew still trailed her.

"I thank ye for yer time, sir, but are ye not the laird's personal guard?"

"Aye, but we've not had a lady to serve in some time." He leaned in as she bent to unhook her hem before she entered the hall. "And the laird seldom rises until *after* the sun." He flashed her a roguish grin as he held the door for her.

She crossed the reed-covered hall, unable to stop her smile. *Truly, the Lord is able to do far more than I ever dreamed or imagined.*

She only prayed her venture into learning the running of the kitchen would go with as much ease.

The kitchen buzzed with chatter, the rhythmic thump of a chopping knife against the cutboard, and the scrape of a spoon against a bowl. But all went silent when they saw who entered. All four women fell quiet and curtsied low.

"My lady, how may we serve ye?" Molly asked as she straightened and brushed her apron.

"Please continue what ye were doing. I didn't mean to upset yer work. Aleen, Rachel, Tara, please continue as if I weren't here."

The women looked at one another. Molly brushed her hand over her apron again. "My lady?"

"I don't want to make a mess of things. Me time here will help me know how matters work. It is a chance to learn. Please continue. I'll sit over here out of the way. Ye won't know I'm even here."

One maid snorted.

Davina fought to stay put. She belonged here. Fergus wanted her to oversee the running of the manse. The kitchen was at the heart of it. She needed to know what went on here. It would be against Fergus' wishes for her to run and hide. She couldn't.

"As ye wish." Molly waved for the other women to continue but the rhythm of the room had changed. The talking slipped to quiet infrequent whispers.

Davina slid onto the stool in the corner near the opening leading to servants' chambers. Though only Rachel slept there. Aleen, Tara, and Molly slept in the homes they shared with their husbands. Only Rachel was unmarried and stayed inside the keep's back chambers.

As they prepared porridge, bread, and cheeses and moved the items to serving trays, Davina slipped from her stool.

Molly squared her narrow shoulders and brushed her hands on her apron again. A few inches taller than Davina, she straightened. "Something displeases ye, my lady?"

"Saints alive, no. Whatever could be the matter with such a well-run kitchen? And the food is always well prepared and tasty."

Molly relaxed but a little. "Forgive me for saying so, my lady, but ye still look displeased."

Davina wasn't going about this right. Izbeil had admonished her not to go messing with things. "Confused. I might be a wee bit confused. But ye've done nothin' wrong."

With a huff, and a near growl, the cook's hands moved to her hips. "And what might be confusin' ye, my lady?"

"Ye're each efficient. Ye work well and quick. Yet …"

One of the cook's hands flicked out toward Davina. "Aye, out with it."

"Tara and Rachel have gone out to the storeroom that is clear on the far side of the gate, more than once, to collect needed ingredients. And, even here in the kitchen, the shelf with the spices and herbs sits on that side of the room while ye all work on this side. 'Tis just me thinking, but would seem to ease yer load if a larder were beside the kitchens and the shelf moved."

Molly threw up her hands and looked at the ceiling. "Praise the Lord above! At last, a body who sees sense." Her arms dropped as she pointed to one maid. "Aleen, after you lay the meal, find Bruce and Stuart. Tell them I've need of their skill." Molly inclined her head toward Davina. "Near a dozen times I've asked me laird for these things. High time someone acted." She gave a curt nod before she returned to her work.

Davina's stomach churned and soured. The food that had been enticing her moments ago now threatened to make her retch. "The laird didn't wish these changes?" She chewed on her bottom lip. Molly didn't answer and Davina fled the kitchens. *What have I done now? I have to find Fergus before things get out of hand.*

Chapter 11

She again ran into Matthew as she flew out the kitchen door.
"Where is the laird?"

"What troubles ye, m'lady?"

Davina's hand pressed to her stomach as her stomach heaved and bile washed the back of tongue. She swallowed hard. "I need to speak with the laird at once."

He waved his hand out for her to continue. "He's in his cabinet."

Her feet couldn't move fast enough, especially considering she didn't know where to go and Matthew followed behind. He knocked on a door that came to block her path at the far end of the passageway opposite the large hall. At Fergus' call, Matthew pushed open the door for her, but again remained without.

"Good morrow, Davina." Fergus glanced up from his papers with a grin.

"Forgive me, sir." She wanted to kneel before him, if only to stop her legs from quaking. "I've gone against yer will and upset the entire manse."

"Davina."

She couldn't stop shaking or her words from tumbling in an endless stream. "I'm so very sorry. 'Twas only a question. An observation. Oh saints, I didn't mean to cause trouble."

Fergus stood. His chair scraped across the stones. His hands rose before her. "Davina, stop!"

She cringed, head bowed low, and eyes pinched closed. Every muscle strained tight, waiting for the blow.

Gentle fingers pulled at her clenched hands. He held one hand, caressing the back with his thumb, as his other hand cradled her cheek. "Davina, lass. Be at peace."

She searched his face but found no anger. "Forgive—"

"Stop!"

She flinched, and he looked to stifle a sigh as he pursed his thin lips together.

"Ye are the—" He paused and waited for her to finish his words.

"—the lady of the manse," she said at last.

He nodded as his smile grew. "Aye. And ye may go anywhere and—"

"—do anything that brings me pleasure, but—"

His gentle fingers brushed her lips to prevent her from speaking. "I'll hear naught more of what ye think an error, lass. Tell me what ye have decided."

She sighed against his touch and fought the tremor racing down her spine. "I went to the kitchen this morn. I only intended to watch. To learn how Molly and the maids worked. But Molly thought I was unhappy with their efforts. I wasn't, Fergus. Molly does a fine job."

"Aye, that she does. So, what bothered ye, then?" Fergus remained patient. His voice a calm coax. This continued touch, something straight from heaven itself.

"There is much time wasted goin' to the storeroom for supplies and across the room for the herbs and spices."

Fergus laughed. "Ah, Molly has found a champion to get her shelf moved."

"And a larder built. I'm sorr—"

His fingers cut off her words again. "It's not that I didn't wish these things, lass. They were not a priority, and I saw not the need. But if ye say they would be a good thing, then they shall be done."

"Molly has already asked Bruce and Stuart to begin."

Fergus moved beside her and raised his arm for her to take. "Good. Things are well in hand."

As they entered the hall, he waved over Owen. "Lady Davina has ordered some improvements to the kitchens. See all who may assist are on the project."

"Aye, my laird." The steward winked at her. "Molly has to be over the moon."

Fergus chuckled as he led her up the steps. "See, all is well. Each day ye bring more joy to me kirth and kin, lass."

After the prayer, they took their places at the high table. Davina nipped at her lip as Fergus filled her plate. "Then, it wouldn't upset ye to know Matthew has been attending me all morn, and he insisted Quinn fashion me some boots?"

"Ye have no boots?" The tray tipped and the food slid to one side before Fergus righted it. "But Crom is a tanner." He growled. "The more I learn of the man, the more I hate him." He filled her plate and bowl. "What have ye been wearing?"

"Me house slippers."

"Fie, lass. No wonder ye were worried about the mud. Right silly thin' to go traipsin' about our sodden soil in naught but slippers. Had I known, Davina, I'd have had Quinn come to ye at once."

"It was nothing—"

"Nothin'?" His head shook. "He treated in such an horrid manner for so long, lass. Ye think ye deserve naught better. I'm of a mind to give Crom a good lashin' the next I see him."

She placed her hand on his arm. He stopped and looked at her.

"Thank ye, Fergus."

"No call to thank a man for forgettin' his duty of the proper care of his kin."

"Yer kindness." She swallowed her threatening tears. "Ye are ever kind and thoughtful, and as ye said, ye didn't know me need."

He left his feasting knife in a hunk of cheese. "Davina, ye must promise me ye'll not go in want again. Ye need not ask me permission. If ye have need, see 'tis met."

She couldn't stop her tears any longer. She brushed one away. "Thank ye again, Fergus."

He squeezed her hand. "Keep yer promise and stop frettin'. We're blessed to have ye here."

Davina ate the rest of her meal through her tears. *Thank ye, Lord. Fergus is a good husband.*

As they stood to leave, they passed Nathair's empty seat. "I wonder what that boy is up to now," Fergus said with a groan.

"I believe he is sleeping off a bit too much drink."

They stopped at the bottom of the dais, and his brow arched as he looked at her.

Davina shrugged. She didn't mean to speak ill of Fergus' son, but her husband already seemed to know the manner of man Nathair was. "We met on the stairs early this morn. He was unsteady and reeked of liquor."

Fergus straightened as much as he could. His eyes widened and his gaze swept over the hall until it landed on his personal guard. "And ye say Matthew attended ye all morn?"

Davina nibbled at her lip. "I suggested he return to ye."

His stare was hard on her again. "What did Nathair do?"

"Nothin', sir."

His voice was steel. "Nothin'? Yet Matthew didn't leave yer side?"

She shook her head. "Matthew didn't go in the kirk or the kitchens, but remained at the doors."

"I asked ye again, Davina. What did Nathair do?"

She placed her other hand on his and squeezed it. "Nathair did naught more than try to block me path. He was too ale-washed to do more. But in me hurry to be free of his smell, I descended the stairs in a rather reckless manner. Matthew saved me from a fall, and again when I stumbled in the yard. I think he feared if he didn't stay close, I would injure meself."

His gaze returned to Matthew, who now looked up with a nod. "I wager not. I'll have a talk with Matthew."

Davina's shoulders sank. "Please don't be angry with him."

Fergus patted her hand. His voice was again gentle. "Ye're frettin' again, lass. Now, I think ye have buildin' to oversee. I shall have a wee talk with Matthew."

Fergus waved the man to follow as he left her and turned toward his cabinet.

Chapter 12

"Matthew, tell me of yer morn." Fergus waved a hand for his guard to sit across the desk from him.

Matthew spoke before he settled. "Lady Davina came careenin' down the stairs as if the devil himself were on her heels." He held his laird in a steady gaze.

"She told me Nathair blocked her path. Did he do more?"

Matthew shrugged one shoulder. "She said the same to me, m'laird."

"But ye stayed with her."

Matthew worked to loosen his tight jaw as his gaze narrowed. "I've made me feelin's clear about yer boy. I'll not see him hurt our lady."

Fergus nodded. "But ye take Davina at her word that Nathair didn't harmed her?"

"It seems he only frightened her this time, but no, he didn't harm her. *Yet*, m'laird"

Fergus nodded and leaned back in his chair with a sigh. "I trust ye to watch over her."

Matthew inclined his head and gave his oath before leaving.

Fergus read over his missive once more. 'Twas time he assured Davina's safety, though it would break his heart and most likely turn the entire manse against him.

"Oh, by the saints," Davina sighed as she plopped down on a slim seat below one of her windows.

"Ye were busy today, m'lady. Ye were." Izbeil filled her cleaning bowl from the pitcher and pulled her night rail from a drawer below it.

"I can't ken how tiring deciding where to place one shelf can be. It is as if I had felled the tree and planed the wood meself, for as addled and sleepy as I am." Davina covered a yawn with the back of her hand. "Gracious."

"Well, ye've made cranky ol' Molly happier than a lass with a new beau. Ye have." Izbeil removed the plaits in Davina's hair and unlaced her gown.

Davina yawned again. "I don't ken which made her happier, the shelf or the larder." Davina had done much harder work growing up under Crom. Even the spinning and weaving she'd learned had been more demanding of her physical strength than deciding on the proper placement of a shelf and a storage closet. But never had the decisions been on her shoulders. Never did she have to balance the desires of those under her with the expense of labor and supplies. And though she tried to be obedient, she still fretted over Fergus' genuine wishes and whether he wanted these improvements done.

She yawned again as Izbeil snuffed out all but one of her candles before she pulled the curtain around her bed closed. Davina had planned to add buttons and loops to more of the dresses, but sleep beckoned and she couldn't refuse.

Something woke Davina. No light shone around the edge of her curtains. Surely it wasn't morning yet. Davina rolled onto her back.

Someone stood at the foot of her bed. The black outline of the dark form was distinct from the curtains.

"Who's there?"

Truly she saw someone, didn't she? She parted the curtains beside her and reached for the candle, but it was out. She opened the fabric wider, hoping a sliver of moonlight from the open shutters would aid her.

No one was there. There was no movement. No click of the closing door. Not that she could have heard anything over the ruckus beat of her erratic heart.

"Fergus?" Her voice choked. Davina had no moisture in her mouth to swallow. She considered getting up, relighting the candle, and searching her chambers. Something kept her snug beneath her bedding. She knew it hadn't been her husband in her room. She'd only known him a few days, but he was a man of his word, and he'd never frighten her.

She eased back on the pillow and quaked at every noise—though she was sure she imagined most of them. She lay awake for what felt like hours and leapt near out of her skin when Izbeil entered before the sun.

"Is all ta right, m'lady? Ye look like ye've seen a spirit. Ye do."

She pushed a smile to her lips, but when her maid raised a brow, Davina turned to gaze out the window as the night slowly gave way to the day. "I didn't sleep well."

"Well, 'tis a new day. It is. All will be better in the light. Ye'll see."

Davina brushed her arms against the chill and prayed it was so.

ChapTer 13

The Lord's day message stirred Fergus' soul this morning. "That was some message, Brother Patrick." He greeted his monk on the kirk steps as he and Davina left.

"'Twas inspired by our sister." Patrick smiled at Davina and her eyes widened.

"Aye, ye." Patrick turned back to Fergus and talked as they made their way to the morning meal together. A couple inches taller than Fergus, now that age had so bent his frame, he had to look up at the holy man.

Patrick spoke with awe and a hint of pride in Davina. "She comes every morn to give thanks to the Lord on bended knee. Then she serves her people with a humble and kind spirit. Such a fine example for us all."

They parted ways, and Fergus led Davina to the high table where Nathair slouched. The emotions warring within Fergus surged from his joy in Davina's growing place in Seycoll to his constant irritation at his wayward son. Nathair had not been inside the kirk—on the Lord's Day or otherwise—in years. "I wish that one would follow yer example, lass." Fergus muttered as they stood behind their seats.

Davina shook her head. "Brother Patrick's words were more than kind, but he couldn't have meant—"

It didn't matter how often or how many people praised her. Davina had spent years being told she was of no worth. She couldn't accept their heart-felt praise now. He patted her hand as they waited for the hall to quiet for the prayer. "My monk is not in a habit of sayin' untruths, lass. Ye're everythin' he said, and so much more." If only his words could get past all the lies and reach her heart.

She stared at him. "Ye sound sad, Fergus."

He shook off the melancholy blanketing him. She was here now and he would not mourn what would happen in the coming weeks. "'Tis nothing."

Fergus noticed her watching him during the meal. He did his best to allay her fears as he told her stories of his youth and made her laugh. Such a profound change had overtaken her in the few days in his home. She didn't search the floor for the mysteries of life, but looked up and out at the world around her. Davina spoke, ever with sweetness and kindness, instead of cowering, waiting to be ordered. Though Crom never provided a formal education for her, she was intelligent and thoughtful in all she did.

Again, sadness weighed on him.

She, of course, noticed. "Are ye sure nothing troubles ye, Fergus?"

"I have work to return to and will miss our time together. 'Tis all, lass."

Her brows pinched her fair skin together and her ice-blue eyes searched his. "Ye sound as if I'll be leagues away and not mere feet."

He took her hand and kissed it, causing another twist of her features as a brow rose high. If only he were a younger man. "As Brother Patrick said, yer mere presence never fails to inspire those around ye, lass. We all lack when ye are not near." His words cracked like a young man growing into manhood. He stood and excused himself before he told her more.

The dark passageway chilled him, and his quiet cabinet screamed his betrayal of her. "But 'tis for her best," he argued back. He sunk into his chair and cradled his face in his hands.

Davina watched Fergus leave. Something troubled him. It was clear as the nose on his face. Maybe she had displeased him. He said otherwise, but … She bit at her lower lip.

Several of the men who worked on the addition of the larder that began with digging a cellar under the kitchen stood and headed in that direction. She followed them. "What are ye doing?"

Bruce turned to her and tipped his head as he stared at her. "There's work to be done on the buildin' ye ordered, m'lady."

She put her hands on her hips. "Not on the Lord's Day."

"Ye want us to wait?"

"They're not to work today?" Molly's curt tone again punctuated her voice. She stood behind Bruce near the blacken kettle hanging over a low fire.

Davina shook her head. "None are to work on the Sabbath."

"But the food—" Rachel looked to the other maid.

"We have plenty of bread baked and much cheese. Prepare a simple stew and leave it to simmer. As long as someone tends the flame and stirs it from time to time, it will cook with little need for someone to stay in the kitchen. All the maids can take turns seeing to the flame to require less of each of you. The Lord gave us a day of rest and commanded we should observe it. Go. Out with ye now. Find yer kin and tell them 'tis the Lord's Day and there is to be no hard labor. Only do what must be done."

It took more shooing, but she at last manage to clear the kitchen of all but Molly, who worked to set the stew and promised to leave in a few moments.

With new purpose, Davina strolled across the near empty hall and down the passageway.

"Enter," Fergus called at her rap on his door.

"Fergus, 'tis the Sabbath."

He looked up from his papers and stared at her. "Aye."

"'Tis a day of rest."

"But business of the manse—"

"Can wait for the morrow. It will still be there. A few hours being obedient to the Lord's command can do no harm. May we go for a ride?"

He sat back in his chair and stared at her.

Her breathing grew shallow, and her lip slipped between her teeth. At some point, she was going to push the man too far. Perhaps today was that time.

A smile grew across his face. "Find Izbeil and see if she knows where Lady S"le's riding clothes are. I'll meet ye in the stables in half an hour."

Davina near skipped from the room.

Dressed in a wide-skirted arisaid, Davina struggled to find a comfortable rhythm atop her garron pony. Both Fergus and Matthew offered assistance as she struggle to master the art of riding alone.

They ventured across the small strip connecting their home to the mainland and up onto the vast expanse of tall waving grass bordered to the west by a large crop of trees.

Fergus pointed to the tree line. "We do much of our hunting there. Would ye care to see some trails?"

"Please." Davina shifted her weight, again catching the plaid under her. It jerked her head and pulled at her hair. In frustration, she yanked the long strip of cloth off her shoulders and her head. She balled it up and set it in her lap with a huff.

Matthew and Fergus laughed. Fergus drew his horse alongside hers. "A lady's plaid is far wider and longer than a man's and mine often annoys me in a similar manner."

She turned to smile at him, but at that moment her pony jerked under her. It threw back its head with a loud whinny and reared up. Davina screamed and snatched up handfuls of mane to keep from being thrown.

The creature landed back on his front hooves so hard, she almost pitched forward over his neck. Before she could find a secure seat again, the frantic animal bolted toward the trees. One foot free of the stirrup and askew in the saddle, Davina clung to the pony the best she could. Unfortunately, in her removal of the plaid and frantic grab for the mane, she had released the reins. They flew out in the wind created by the crazed creature's escape. She thought to reach for one, but as the pony darted between trees, it was all she could do to hang on.

Fergus and Matthew shouted behind her, but their words were lost under the drum of hooves and her heartbeat thundering in her ears. She caught glimpses of them as they raced between the trees beside her to get ahold of her fleeing mount.

She shrieked again as the pony brushed too close to a tree. The rough bark tore at her shoulder and hair. Another near miss and they burst out into the open. Matthew appeared in her path, causing her pony to veer to the side and slam her into Fergus.

A powerful arm encircled her waist. "Let go, lass. I have ye."

The pony continued on as Matthew ran it down. Davina sat with her back pressed against Fergus' chest. She couldn't decide whose heart beat harder.

"Davina, are ye hale, lass?" Fergus' breathy question caressed her sweaty neck.

"I think so. What made him take off like that?"

"An arrow in his rump!"

They both turned to Matthew, who was leading her pony back. "Arrow?" She and Fergus said at the same time.

Matthew brought the animal alongside them. The fetching protruded only a wee bit above the trickle of blood running down his flank.

"Poor thing," Davina said. She reached out to stroke the injured animal and winced.

"Ye're bleeding too, lass." Fergus brushed her hair aside.

"Is it bad?" Matthew moved to the other side of Fergus for a better look.

"Nay, scratches from a tree." Fergus turned his mount around. "Best get ye back and tended, so it doesn't become worse, though."

Fergus' arms encircled her waist as her legs dangled over his right thigh. She could feel the hardened muscles beneath his tunic. He was still a formidable man. No one had hugged her since Mum died. It was a comfort she'd forgotten, and she never wanted him to let her go.

She laid her head on his shoulder, and he groaned. She pulled from him. "I'm hurting ye."

He shook his head. "'Tis been long since I held a bonny lass in me arms." He eased her back into him again. "Rest, lass. We'll be back in Seycoll soon."

"Who would shoot an arrow at one of our ponies?" Every muscle in Fergus' body tightened at her question. He and Matthew exchanged a long glance. But neither spoke. Davina shuddered in their silence.

"Don't fret, lass. Was probably just a stray bolt of a careless hunter."

The look Matthew gave Fergus said a hundred things she didn't understand, but she didn't think either of them believed the laird's words.

Chapter 14

Davina woke again to someone standing at the end of her bed. She reached for the candle. But though she had shielded it from any wind, the candle had gone out. It sat dark on the table beside her bed. She drew the bedding up to her chin and strained to listen to every sound. If only she could go to her husband and have him hold her the way he had while they rode back to the manse.

The next night, she wedged a chair under the door to the hall and the other door that Izbeil had once said led to the laird's chambers. When both doors sat secure, she slept well.

Bang! Oof! "M'lady?"

Davina scrambled out of bed and rubbed her eyes. She moved the chair and opened the door for Izbeil.

"What in heaven's name…?" The maid scanned the room and saw the other chair.

"Forgive me. I overslept." Davina snatched up her plaid to cover herself.

Izbeil surveyed the room. "What's happened?"

"Nothin'."

Arms akimbo, Izbeil scowled at her. "Out with it. Speak the truth."

Davina moved to stare at the ocean from her window. "'Tis naught to worry about. I'm sure it was all in me imaginings."

"Ye can't hide at yer window this time, m'lady. I'll not let ye. I won't." When Davina wouldn't speak, Izbeil turned her. "Forgive me, but somethin' has frightened ye enough to warrant barrin' yerself in. Tell me what ye think ye imagined."

"Two nights I've woken, and it looked as if someone stood at the foot of me bed."

Izbeil gasped. "Sakes alive. Who was it?"

"I don't know. The candle was out."

"That's not good. Not good at all. No wonder ye've looked so tired. Poor dear." Izbeil ushered her into the washroom. "Come. We'll clean ye and start a new day."

"Where are the boys with the water?"

Izbeil chuckled. "Bruce needed them to help fell trees to secure the cellar. I reckoned ye wouldn't mind missing one bath."

Davina smiled. "Perhaps we can make it a practice for me to only have a full bath a few times a week."

Izbeil shrugged. "We shall see." She turned Davina around. "Yer shoulder is healing fine. Right fine indeed."

With her late start, she had little time for more than her prayers before she met Fergus at the high table.

"We are expectin' an honored guest three days hence." His voice spoke with excitement, but it didn't reach his eyes.

Davina nibbled at her lip. Another task she could fail at. "What do ye require to make him feel welcome?"

"Fresh reeds in the hall, the guest chamber on the second floor readied, and full meals while Laird Hew of the clan Ross stays with us.

We enjoy rather simple fare most days, but while the laird is here, I wish to give him proper honor."

"All will be prepared as ye instructed, Fergus. I'll see to it." It seemed easy enough.

Fergus patted her hand. "Assign staff to the tasks. Ye're not to be doin' it yerself."

She nodded. It would have been easier to do it herself than command the staff to see to everything. She took a slow breath. "Is Laird Hew a friend?"

"Aye."

She continued to stare as her stomach rolled. "Ye don't seem happy to welcome him."

Did Fergus sigh? "It has been long since we entertained anyone."

"All will be ready. I assure ye." It would be, even if she had to do it. What would Fergus do if she went against his orders? She shuddered.

"I would expect nothin' less from ye, Davina."

Fresh rushes added a clean scent to the hall. The lads from the stables had worked hard yesterday. The maid had scrubbed the chamber Laird Hew would use clean. They would add fresh linens today. Now Davina need to check with Molly on the meals.

"Good morn, Molly."

The kitchen that hummed with noise most days was as quiet as a tomb. Molly, Tara, and Aleen jumped when she entered. Where was Rachel? Davina followed each gaze as it moved to the chambers hidden in the rear of the kitchens.

A muffled yelp came from the darkness. Fabric rent.

Rachel. Saints save them, someone was having a go at her. While the other maids worked in here, someone acted with brazen boldness to attack Rachel only feet away.

Davina looked at Molly and mouthed "Nathair," without making a sound. Molly answered with several small nods.

Davina had to do something. A courageous act with no fear, but could she even do that? She quaked and stepped to intervene. But stopped after only two steps. She couldn't confront the man. He was far too strong for her and, by their current behavior it was clear the maids would do nothing to interfere with the laird's son. But she had to do something. She was the lady of the manse. These people were in her care. She could abandon none of them to Nathair's cruelty. *Lord, give me wisdom and help us.*

Another stifled scream.

Davina couldn't stand to do nothing. These were her people. She steeled herself and filled her words with all the bravery and command she could call forth. "Rachel, come here. I have need of yer assistance."

There was shuffling.

"Hurry, lass." She made her words as sharp as Crom's.

Rachel appeared moments later, sliding her gown up over her shoulder. An angry blotch screamed on her cheek and her eyes were red with tears.

Davina ignored it all and turned to Molly. "I shall only borrow her for a spell. It shant be long."

"The maids are yers to command." Molly tried to keep the usual edge in her voice, but relief tainted her words.

Davina waved Rachel to follow her to the door into the hall when Nathair appeared from the dark opening. He straightened his clothes and glared at her.

Lord help! She startled at his presence; her hand landing on her throat with a gasp. "Nathair, what are ye—" She waved him out the back door. "We've no plans for improvements in the servants' chambers, man." She continued to shoo him. "All the work is outside. Out with ye now. The maids have much to do afore Laird Hew arrives. They can't have ye under foot. Out with ye!"

The instant she closed the outer door on him, she whirled on her heel. Molly opened her mouth to speak, but Davina raised her hand for her to hold her tongue. She flew across the room, snatched up Rachel's hand, and pulled her into the hall.

"Matthew, follow us." The man snapped straight at her command.

The women moved toward the keep stairs. "Up with ye, Rachel. To the top. Hurry." Spotting her maid at the far end of the hall, Davina yelled. "Izbeil, come now!" She fled up the stairs behind Rachel as heavy steps followed.

Davina ushered Rachel inside her chambers and waited for Izbeil to enter before she turned to Matthew with her voice low. "Nathair had a go at Rachel. Guard this door, please."

He growled as his gaze hardened. "Aye!"

Davina slipped inside and secured the door with the chair. She ignored Izbeil's confused stare and led Rachel to the stool. She knelt before the lass, who couldn't be over two years younger than her. Davina brushed her thick brown hair away and caressed her wounded cheek. "Did he …"

"Nay, m'lady. Ye stopped him in time." Her tears started again.

Davina cradled her close and stroked her hair.

Izbeil stepped beside them with a deep scowl. "M'lady."

"Don't scold me on what's proper. Nathair attacked Rachel, and I don't care what a lady ought not do."

"Is she hurt?" Izbeil whispered.

"He left scratches on her. Do we have a little more of the ointment we put on my shoulder? Nathair's always filthy."

Izbeil moved to the bathing chamber and returned a moment later. She didn't allow Davina to clean the wounds or apply it, so Davina contented herself with continuing to rock the sobbing girl.

"Izbeil, do I reckon rightly that now Nathair has taken it in his mind to have her, he'll not stop till he succeeds?"

Izbeil groaned. "Ye speak the right of it. Ye do."

Davina set her jaw as a notion bloomed. "Then she can't remain here."

Rachel jerked in her arms, and Davina released her, brushing her hair from her face again. "I know 'tis a terrible thing, but ye must be safe, Rachel. I'll not let him—"

Rachel interrupted. "Thank ye, m'lady."

She held Rachel's hands. "I think I would die if I had to leave Seycoll, but it won't be forever. This I promise ye. I'll find a way to bring ye back when 'tis safe."

Izbeil moved toward the door. "Me Duncan will know what to do. He will."

Davina reached for the ointment. "Tell Matthew what we plan and go to Duncan. We must work in haste."

Chapter 15

Against her protests, Izbeil forced Davina from her own rooms. The maid wouldn't allow her to continue to stoop and care for the frightened Rachel. Davina had done what she could. Now, the staff would see to the rest.

Matthew and Angus stood outside when she exited. "I'll go with ye. Angus will watch the women," Matthew said with a nod.

Davina's brow rose.

Matthew waved her to proceed down the stairs. "Angus is smitten with Rachel. He'll not let anything more happen to her."

Davina stood in the great hall for a moment, at a loss as to what to do. She'd found a new strength and courage she didn't know she had. Could she hang onto it? She turned to the kitchens. This time, Matthew came in with her.

Davina clung to her courage. "What may I do to help, Molly?"

Molly's fists perched on her hips. "'Help?' The lady does not *help* in the kitchen."

"Never knew a noblewoman who was of any use cookin'," Tara snorted.

Davina laughed. "We are all a rather useless lot to be sure, but I can clean a pot and slice vegetables, too. Though I'm sure not as fine as ye."

Molly sputtered and fussed with her apron. "Ye can't."

"Saints alive, why not? I offered. Ye didn't ask. Yer shorthanded, and we have a guest who will be here on the morrow." Davina moved to the peg and pulled down Rachel's apron. She put it on as she walked back toward Molly. "Please, let me be of some use. Izbeil has banned me from assisting Rachel further. I need something to occupy meself."

"As ye wish." Molly wagged a finger at her. "But ye'll not be scrubbing pots."

Davina inclined her head, and Aleen handed her a knife and some carrots. "Thank ye, m'lady."

Davina didn't understand all the fuss. "'Tis just a little chopping."

Aleen's voice shook. "Nay. For Rachel. Thank ye for saving her."

Davina focused on her chopping. She didn't need to cut her fingers and prove how useless she could be. "Thank the Lord I came when I did and He gave me the strength to do it."

"Amen," all three women answered.

Fergus brushed the flank of the pony Davina had ridden and inspected the wound. Good. It healed well. He'd hate for the creature to be put down.

Matthew stormed into the stable.

"Ah, Matthew, have ye seen Duncan?"

"M'laird." The square of his shoulders and the tenor of his voice said there was trouble.

Fergus gave his guard his full attention. "What's happened?"

Matthew stepped outside and moved to a deserted place before he spoke in hushed tones. "Nathair attacked Rachel. In the kitchen chambers as all the staff stood without. He grows bolder."

Fergus sagged against the wall. "Has anyone tended her?"

"Our lady stopped it. Rachel has a few scratches from his groping hands and will no doubt suffer the remembrance for far too long, but she is otherwise unharmed."

"Davina?" Straightening, Fergus almost grabbed Matthew and shook him. "Why are ye not watching her? He'll come for her next."

"I think he already has. For now, I've been told Nathair has ridden out of the manse. Angus watches our lady nonetheless. She works in the kitchen."

Fergus' long strides carried him across the soft dirt to the hall. "She works like a common maid? And Nathair has harmed her? Explain."

Matthew pulled him up short. "Iz told me our lady believes someone has been in her chambers staring at her from the foot of the bed. She's taken to wedgin' chairs under the latches to thwart entry."

"Have bars installed at once. We need to see to Rachel's safety as well. Nathair will not let her be now."

"Rachel's welfare has been seen to. Duncan carries her away to a place of safety."

Fergus nodded and started up the outer stairs to enter the keep.

"M'laird, if I may speak freely?" Matthew took two stairs at a time to keep pace. "When ye have another heir, Nathair could be set aside for a better man."

With a sigh, Fergus waved the man back to his cabinet. "There is something ye must know."

Chapter 16

"Davina!"

Davina released her startled breath. "Saints alive, m'laird. Ye startled me, and I nearly cut meself. Blood or worse, the tip of me finger, in the meal would not be appealing to yer honored guest."

He stood on the other side of the cutboard from where she worked. "Ye'll stop this at once. Come, Davina."

"There is much to do and Molly now has little help. Rachel—"

He took the knife from her and slammed it down. "I'm aware. Heather will be assistin' now."

Davina tried to retrieve the knife. "Heather? But she has so many bairns to care for, m'laird."

"Davina, ye will come now." He stretched out his arm toward her.

She had reached the point she feared. She pushed him one too many times. Wiping her hands on the apron, she bowed her head. "Aye, m'laird." She handed Aleen the apron and took Fergus' arm. He led her to the cabinet in silence. Matthew trailed behind. He looked sad. Gracious, how mad was Fergus with her?

"Sit."

She dropped into the chair and fiddled with a ribbon on the bodice of her gown.

"Are ye hale, lass?" His hushed voice dripped with concern, not rage.

His kind words caused her to look up. She nodded.

He brought her a cup of mead before taking his seat behind the desk. "Tell me what happened."

Fergus stood and paced when she finished. "Ye never confronted Nathair? Never accused him of attacking Rachel?"

"Nay, m'laird." Did that please him?

Fergus stopped behind his chair. He gripped the back with a fearsome hold. "And ye're not sure it was he in yer room at night?"

By the saints, how did he know about that? "I couldn't see a face."

He paced again and muttered more to himself than direct the question at her. "But who else would dare?"

"I'm sorry, m'laird. I didn't mean—" Davina squirmed in her seat.

He jerked to a stop and slammed his fist on his desk, making her jump. "I told ye once, Davina, don't apologize for him." A guttural growl exploded from his chest. "Ye did right in handlin' him the way ye did, lass. But I still have no grounds to take to the king."

"Take to the king?"

"I will not have Nathair take over the manse when I'm gone. He is unworthy, as ye witnessed today. But I must have cause to reject him. The king wants loyal clans to control his land. I need proof Nathair is not that man. But as ye never accused him and Rachel is now away to safety, I have no grounds against him—again."

"Molly and the maids—"

Fergus turned from her with a shake of his head. His words filled with the weight of his son's horrid behavior. "The women will not speak against him for the fear Nathair will harm them next."

Davina chewed on her lip.

Fergus came around the desk toward her. "Ye did right. I don't blame ye, lass. I blame me own weakness for not puttin' a stop to him sooner. The love of a father for his son is an odd beast."

He remained a little apart from her. Davina remembered his muscular arms about her when he'd rescued her from the pony. She needed that now. Just to be held for a moment. She'd comforted Rachel. Would it be too much to ask the same of the husband who would never know her as a true wife?

He straightened with a steeled resolve. "Matthew and Angus are yer guards now. Ye are to go nowhere without one of them. Bars are bein' built into yer doors. Ye'll be safe." It was a command.

She stood and took a tentative step toward him. A moment to be held; that was all she needed. "Thank ye, Fergus."

He turned from her and back to his paperwork. "I don't want ye workin' like a common maid again, Davina. Ye're the—"

"The lady of the manse. Aye." She sighed and left.

Matthew embodied the same downcast spirit consuming her. "Perhaps a walk on the wall overlookin' the ocean will help ease ye, m'lady," he offered in a hopeful whisper.

The salt-kissed wind did not replace her husband's arms. She found no solace in the gulls or waves. She turned to prayer. *Lord, please watch over Rachel. Let her find joy, comfort, and peace wherever she may light this night. Watch over those who remain. Keep Yer children safe and bring into the light all the schemes of those who plot evil.*

Even prayer didn't bring an end to her melancholy.

The laughter of several young boys drew her attention. They played shinty. Their long sticks smacked a ball toward the nets on either end of the open area below her. She eased down the stairs, watching them. Their joy was so powerful, it almost touched her aching soul.

"Da ye wanna to play, m'lady?" Young Rory offered her his stick.

She leaned down. "Ye'll have to teach me how."

"Okay. Hold the camen like this." They helped her place her hands on the stick and guide it toward the ball.

One boy who was on her team took the pass and moved the ball toward their net.

"Come, m'lady, ye must help us score." They raced across the grass together. The ball came back her way when an opponent hit it away from the net.

She swung and missed, not even getting close. The ball raced over her toes and past her. "Oh, no."

The boys laughed. "It's okay, m'lady. We do that all the time. 'Tis a wily wee ball."

The orb batted back and forth; at one point, it got lost under her skirts.

"That's na fair, m'lady. Ye can't go hidin' it."

She stepped away with care not to disturb the ball. "It may not be fair, lad, but seems as I can only hit it when the little bugger is still."

The boys laughed, and she gave it a good whack. It sped toward the goal, only to be slowed by the grass before it reached the prize. A teammate tapped it in.

Half the boys gave up a cheer. "Told ye our lady would be good luck."

"We didn't argue with ye, Rory. We all know that."

Davina straightened took a deep breath and smiled. "Thank ye, for lettin' me play."

Rory took the camen back. "Maybe ye could play again?"

"Next time, she's on our team," the other boys said before they all ran off.

Davina sat on a step and shook a pebble from her boot. "Please don't tell the laird. Oh heavens, and don't go telling Izbeil. They'll scold me for sure for not 'acting the lady'." She stood and looked at Matthew. "A child's laughter is medicine for the soul."

"Aye, it is." Sadness still shaded his eyes.

She turned toward the keep. "I imagine not as good a medicine as when they're yer own bairns." The gloom seeped back in, adding weight to her feet.

"True, m'lady." Honestly, the man sounded as though he heard her own aching heart. "Don't despair, there will be a time for ye, too."

If only that were true.

The great hall was quieter than normal. A deep pallor blanketed the entire room. Nathair wasn't present, which was always a reason to celebrate. Several people bowed their heads to her in respect.

She found a bit of her mettle again as she approached the laird at the high table. "Fergus, ye must brighten the mood."

"They've all heard what me son did. There is naught to make merry about," Fergus muttered.

She dared to face him and squeezed his arm. "Rachel is safe. He didn't do what he intended. God's favor on her should be praised and celebrated. He protected His children. Give the Lord His due, Fergus. The rest will be forgotten for now." The words tumbled from her in a bold stream. She chewed on her lip when they at last stopped.

He inclined his head. "Ye're correct, as always, lass."

Fergus called everyone to prayer, praising God for His protection. After they said amen, the room filled with new life. But gazes still flicked to Nathair's seat. There was still much to worry about.

Chapter 17

"M'lady."

Davina exited the kirk the following morning to find Robert waiting with Matthew. The rising sun sparkled off the skin of his scalp through his thinning, light hair. She recalled all she knew about the smithy. He and Molly had grown boys. Their lass had married just before Davina arrived.

His deep bow made his heavy leather apron crinkle with an odd rustle. The smell of the forge hung about him. "I came to thank ye. From the bottom of me heart, I'm right grateful. I owe ye a debt."

"Saints alive, whatever for?" Davina glanced between the still bent smith and Matthew.

"Rachel is me distant kin. She came here hopin' to have a better place in the world. I couldn't protect her, but ye did."

Davina released a quiet breath. "God saved her. I was just thankin' Him for the favor He showed Rachel."

Robert seemed not to hear her. "Whatever ye need, ye have but ask."

"That is kind of ye. I'll bear it in mind." She turned toward the stairs in the wall as he moved in the other direction. "Robert? There may be something."

"Say the words, m'lady. I'm yer man."

"Could ye fashion me a small dirk? Something I could wear on a chain around me waist and hide in the folds of me skirt?"

"Aye. It'd be wise to have somethin' for yer own safety. I know the laird has ye guarded, but best to leave naught to chance. I'll begin on it straight away. A day or two at most, m'lady." He bowed again and hurried off.

"Laird Hew, welcome." Fergus moved across the hall and greeted their guest as Davina waited in front of the dais. *I'm the lady of the manse. The lady.* She repeated the words again and again to shore up her pluck.

Hew was about a score younger than her husband. Stocky build, though he still appeared strong. His ashen brown hair grew sprinkled with strands of white.

The men greeted one another with a hearty grip of their forearms and a thump on the back. Hew's neat plaid lay across his clean tunic and tan breeks.

They spoke with quiet words before moving toward her. "This is Lady Davina."

She curtsied low at Fergus' introduction.

Hew took her hand as she rose and kissed her knuckles. "It is my greatest pleasure to make your acquaintance, my lady." He bowed over her hand and kissed it again.

Davina reclaimed her appendage and slipped closer to Fergus. He hadn't introduced her as his wife, but the visiting laird must understand. "We're honored to welcome ye to our home, m'laird."

Hew's right brow arched high as his gaze shifted to Fergus.

Fergus waved the man forward. "Ye're just in time for midday, Hew. Come, let us eat." Hew's retainers moved to the boards and sat among Seycoll's kin. They greeted several as old friends.

"I'll inform Molly we're ready." Davina moved toward the kitchen, but she could feel Hew's eyes following her. She tried to rub away the chill snaking up her arms.

When she returned, though there was plenty of room at the high table, especially considering Nathair had yet to return, Fergus sat Laird Hew on her other side. She eyed Fergus, but already her weak courage failed. She didn't dare say anything.

Hew tried several times to pull Davina into the conversation. "What do you think of the king's continued endeavors to make war on the English?"

Saints alive. No one ever asked her opinion on what she'd eat or wear, let alone the affairs of the country. She knew nothing of politics. The concerns of the king were surely none of hers. She looked to Fergus for help.

"An Englishman, kin to Hew's mother, fostered him in England from a young age. That's why he's lost his brogue. And why he gives a bugger what happens on our border."

"Is not the security and independence of all of our lands every man's concern?"

Fergus raised a meaty rib towards his mouth. "Men, aye. But the ladies care naught about our warin' ways, Hew." He tore the meat off with his teeth.

Davina poked at the food on her plate, queasy now, caught between the men's conversation.

"You may live hidden on the desolate costal hills of the northernmost Highlands, but if the English come to take our king's throne, there will be no safe place for loyal Scots."

Davina squirmed as desperation grew to excuse herself from the table. The men talking over her of war and the security of the kingdom was both unnerving and quite annoying. Could she fain a headache? In truth, one throbbed a relentless drum in her skull already.

Hew again directed his conversation to her. "My lady, what think you of the talk to build a great university?"

University? What was that? Again, she dared a glance at her husband.

Fergus, at last, came to her aid. "If they build an institution for higher learning, it will lie a full day's ride south, Hew. The lady was reared north in Aberdeen."

Hew speared a hank of meat and cut off several pieces. "I have insisted Cameron attend when it opens."

"Yer boy's well grown and has fought beside our king. Why demand learning at the university so many years in the future?" Fergus stuffed a large slice of boar in his mouth and waited for his friend to reply.

Davina's head throbbed. Would Fergus allow her to return to her chambers? She glanced at him, but he directed her attention back to Hew with a raise of his chin. Both men had meat juices glistening in their beards. This was by far the worst meal she'd endured since she'd arrived near a month ago.

"It is the future, man." Hew smiled at her. "Do you not agree, my lady?"

She swallowed the bit of bread, trying to lodge itself in her parched throat. "Education is always of value, m'laird."

"Value? To be sought after at all costs, I say. It is what separates us from the animals." Hew banged his fist on the boards, rattling their dinnerware and Davina's raw nerves. A momentary hush fell over the hall.

Soon, those gathered below returned to their laughter and conversation and Laird Hew sat waiting, demanding answers to his inquiries of her.

She said little, unsure of what was correct and what the man wanted her to say to ease his stern demeanor. She ate less than normal and her fortitude waned.

Aleen stepped forward and refilled her cup with mead. The men's cups held Fergus' favorite, ale.

Davina acknowledged the welcome break from the men's banter. "Thank ye, Aleen. Please go and enjoy yer meal."

The maid bowed with a knowing grin and left.

Hew snorted. "Servants are to work until their betters have no need of them. And they are never to be thanked. 'Tis their duty."

Davina sputtered and coughed as she tried not to choke. She wiped dark mead from her chin. "Their betters?"

"Yes. They are in a low place in life and only exist to serve." Hew gave a curt nod and returned to his meal.

Fire stirred in her belly, souring what little she had eaten. Davina stood, propelled by the same strength as when she'd called to Rachel. "M'laird, there's naught better about me if I treat me people like the dung on the bottom of me shoe." She descended the stairs and walked to the boards lining the hall below, and a second hush fell over those gathered. Raising her voice so Hew would be sure to hear, she continued. "I'm not better than these fine people merely because I was born who I am. They have skills and talents I could never aspire to. That they have so willingly decide to do things as I may have whim is only a testament to their character. I have no skill to fashion leather, cook an edible meal, bend metal to me will, and I've never studied the Scriptures." She walked between the long trestle tables, acknowledging each person. "These fine kirth and kin have welcomed me with kindness and care. That should not be tread on with disdain. Me sole role is to see to the welfare of these people. If they thrive, then I, too, will live well. I can nay treat them as measly slaves."

She paused before Brother Patrick. "Does not the Word tell us to not think better of ourselves than we ought? To love our brothers and sisters as ourselves and that we will be known as Christ's followers by our love, one for another?"

Patrick's chest puffed until his ribs brushed the table's edge. "Aye, m'lady. Right ye are."

Davina turned her gaze to the high table. Fergus sat still as stone, but his eyes sparkled with joy.

Laird Hew's face grew near the same shade of her hair. "It has been a pleasure to see you again, old friend, but I must be away." Hew's words leaked through is almost still lips.

"Oh?" Fergus coughed up his ale in a sputtering gasp.

Davina approached the table from below. "We have a room prepared for ye," she said, though not really loud enough for either man to hear her.

"I'll not be taking you up on your offer, Fergus." Hew stomped toward the door and nodded to his men. Fergus followed close on his heels. They stopped and talked at the door. Hew's gaze fell upon her where she still stood near the dais, and he shook his head.

Fergus said something, but again Hew shook his head. Fergus gripped his arm as when they greeted one another and then let Hew leave. He looked tired; his shoulders slumped more than normal.

She met him at the side of the dais. Tears shook her words. "I'm sorry yer friend left without agreeing to yer business, Fergus. I never should have so bold as to speak to your honored guest in such a manner."

He sighed but did not meet her gaze. "Ye spoke with deep wisdom and I'm grateful to ye, lass. 'Tis for the best, I suppose. I know another laird will be agreeable." With a last sad glance at her, he turned and disappeared down the passageway to his cabinet.

CHAPTER 18

Davina didn't see Fergus other than at meals over the next couple of days. He only spoke a few words and ate as little as she did. She'd done wrong in speaking to Hew the way she had. It was clear she'd upset Fergus. But the people of the estate were different.

They smiled, offered to make her anything she desired, and some even dared speak to her as a friend. None asked anything of her, wanting naught more than to shower her with kindness.

"Good morn to ye, m'lady." Robert's boisterous greeting sent chickens scattering and brought her up short.

"Good morn."

He held out a sheathed blade on a long chain. Holding it in one hand, she drew it from the dark leather. The blade was the length of her hand and swirled with an elaborate pattern in the glistening metal. She rested the tip on her finger and drew blood. She sheathed it again and sucked on her finger a moment. "'Tis sharp." She laughed at her own clumsiness.

"Shall protect ye well." Robert bowed again.

Davina wrapped the chain around her waist, letting the blade dangle over her right thigh. It almost lay hidden within the folds of its own. It empowered her to know it was there. More so than Matthew or Angus. "Thank ye, Robert."

"I pray ye never have need of it, m'lady." Robert bowed and returned to his work.

Davina stepped from the crisp fall morning into the flickering light of the kirk. She neared the altar with awe. That God would have brought her to such a place and knit these people in her heart so firmly in only a matter of weeks. Her strength grew. She—

"Where is she?"

Davina whirled on the deep voice. Fear replaced her courage so fast that it made her sway on her feet.

Nathair stepped out of the shadows only enough for her to recognize him. "Where is she?"

Lord. She couldn't think of more. Feigning ignorance would be a waste of time. She could never lie with conviction. She grasped for the pluck she'd shown him before. "I don't know."

Nathair crossed his arm. "I will find where ye have hidden her."

She rooted to her spot and raised her chin. "As I had naught to do with her leaving this place, I shall be of no help to ye."

He sneered. "Ye intend to clear the entire manse of women, lass?"

Heart pounding in her ears, Davina struggled to think. He threatened them all. Married and maiden, none were safe. Her hand covered the weight over her right thigh. Would God forgive her if she hurt another in His house? "I will guard every life put under my care." She let her voice rise and tried to keep out the shrill edge. "Now, Nathair, if ye've come to unburden yer soul …" Both doors opened and Matthew and Brother Patrick stood tall, filling both door frames. She let her volume drop. "I'd be happy to return another time."

Nathair slipped along the far wall at the end of the pews. With slow, heavy steps, he crossed the front of the kirk toward her.

Matthew's hand went to the hilt of his sword.

Patrick moved closer to her too.

Her fingers tightened around her dirk's hilt.

Nathair didn't stop, but leaned in as he passed. "I've not finished with ye."

Davina remained still and on her feet until Nathair left the building. Then her legs gave out. Only Brother Patrick's quick action saved her from landing on the floor.

"M'lady?" Matthew was beside her in two large strides.

She put up her hands to stay him. "I'm unharmed, just startled."

Bother Patrick lowered her to a pew. "Ye've lost all color, sister."

"What'd he say?" Matthew demanded.

Davina shook her head, trying to lock her eyes on the gold cross on the altar. "Naught but a shallow threat to every woman in the manse."

Patrick crossed himself. "I shall petition the Lord for safety at once."

Matthew turned toward the door. "I'll inform the laird."

"Matthew, we must let everyone know our women shall go nowhere alone." Davina couldn't contain her shudder. "Never alone," she wheezed.

At the evening meal that day, only Fergus' silent presence shielded her from Nathair's leering stare.

She rose when Fergus did after the evening meal. "Might we go to the solar?"

"I'm tired, lass." Fergus turned and vanished.

Davina rubbed at her arms and clutched them tightly about her.

"I'd be happy to chase away the chill." Nathair's lip curled.

Davina yelped at Nathair's words in her ear. His foul stench washed over her and threatened to bring up what little dinner she'd eaten.

Matthew stood from his seat just in front of her.

"I just want a place to call home, Nathair. Why can ye not let me be?"

He licked his lips, his eyes raking over her face and down to linger on her bosom. "Ye're such a bonny lass."

She moved away from him, but he seized her wrist in a crushing grip. "Ye're hurting me," she whispered. "The entire hall watches."

"Ye think they will interfere with the laird's son?"

Would they? The people talked as though they favored her. Each was kind—to her face. But how much kindness could overcome the fear of going against the laird and a man who had the power of life and death in his hand?

"I could strip ye bear and lay ye out on this board. None would care. Ye're just a woman. Of no more value than what pleasure ye can provide a man."

"M'lady, ye are looking unwell," Matthew said, stepping to the front of the dais.

Molly stood. Her voice trembled when she spoke. "M'lady, the maids are giving me some trouble. I need ye to talk to them."

"Aye, m'lady. Molly pesters me each night with her struggles in the kitchens. If ye settle the situation, I'd be right grateful." Robert came forward to stand beside Matthew.

Izbeil rounded the corner and stood at the dais stairs. "M'lady, a bath has been drawn for ye to relax in."

It seemed the entire manse wanted her attention at once. She tried to look at Nathair, where he still stood behind her, twisting her wrist and pinning it to her back, causing painful spasms. "Let. Me. Go." She said each word slow and quiet.

He released her with a low growl only she could hear.

She followed Molly to the kitchens first.

"M'lady, we never—" Aleen, Tara, and Heather stammered as one.

Davina waved her quaking hands at them. "Ye are all good, women. A better run kitchen in all the land could nay be found." She braced herself on the cutboard and tried to slow her breathing and pounding heart. "We have to look out for one another."

"Aye, m'lady." Tara reached out and raised Davina's dangling sleeve, revealing the angry welt left behind by Nathair.

"The hall is clear. Come m'lady," Izbeil called from the doorway.

Even with both hands braced against the wall on either side of the stairwell, Davina's trembling legs struggled to carry her up to her chambers. The last of the lads passed them with his empty buckets as they entered her chamber and Izbeil secured the door. Davina staggered and her knees buckled.

"Ye were strong enough to stand up to that wretch and save Rachel. Ye have the strength to face him for yer own safety. Ye do. Come. A hot bath will wash away the thought of him."

Davina soaked until the bath water turned frigid. Dressed in her night rail, alone in her chamber with the doors secure and Angus standing guard without, emotions flooded her. She moved to the door shared with Fergus' room.

She raised her hand to the wood, but only her palm pressed in a silent plea against it. Would he welcome her if she knocked? Just for a moment, would he hold her? No. He had left her alone with *him*. Well, not alone. They were in a hall half-full of their people. But Fergus knew his kin's reluctance to stand against his son.

Ye're a worthless waste. No one wants a useless woman. Her forehead leaned against Fergus' door as Da's words assailed her again. Tears fell, splattered on the floor, and sprinkled her toes. She sank to the floor, never daring to ask for entry or acceptance.

Chapter 19

Fergus had left the hall early, telling Davina he was tired. He was anything but. Fergus paced his chambers until Angus came to tell him of Nathair's accosting the lass. He'd been a fool to leave with the boy so close to her. Fergus had to get her out of here. Boyd said he would come. Would he be a good fit?

For the millionth time, he crossed his chambers to her door. His hand braced against the wood. The cool and rough surface reminded him of his manner toward her of late.

He flung himself away and stomped back across his chamber in the other direction. How could he have known the lass would work into his heart so quick and so deep? His hand brushed over his head. Had he only been a younger man, or had a son worthy of her. No, this was God's punishment for allowing Nathair to degrade into such a despot. He'd lose her and it would tear out his heart.

Davina loved his people. She loved him, even when he spent only a few fleeting moments with her at meals. Having her in the manse had proved a blessings for all of them.

He trudged back to her door and raised his hand to knock. She needed to know what he intended.

Davina's downcast face flooded his vision, driving him back. She would hate him. He couldn't tell her. Only when he had no other choice, would he speak the word that would turn all his kin against him and probably kill him. He rested his forehead against the cool wood. "Forgive me for being a coward, lass," he whispered.

The days grew shorter, and the weather turned as bleak as Davina's mood.

"Good morn, m'lady."

Davina stopped at the back of the hall near the door. "Good morn, Quinn. What has ye up so early and out in this storm?"

The tanner who had fashioned the boots that cradled her feet in such warmth and comfort bowed. Quinn's grin spread across his face; he wore his brown hair pulled back in a warrior's knot. His eyes all but danced as he looked at her. "Ye, m'lady."

"Saints alive, forgive me."

Quinn cocked his head to the side and stared at her. "I bring ye a present."

To tell the man of her unworthiness would be an affront to his offer. To refuse would wound his generosity and his pride. Her lip wedged itself between her teeth to keep her from saying anything to mar his kindness.

He picked up a leather bundle and handed it to her with a nod. "Our winters can get a bit soggy and I know ye favor a visit to the kirk each morn."

She unfolded a long leather cape. It must have taken many hides to fashion. He'd oiled it to keep out the water, like the tall boots he'd made her. Impressed into the back and the skirt were vines and intricate flowers in various stages of blooming. "Never have I seen such work in a simple cloak. 'Tis beautiful." Her hand brushed over the surface and tears stung her eyes. "Ye're too kind." Her voice cracked.

"We know ye pray over each of us by name, m'lady. Least I can off is to see ye there and back dry."

Oh, how she wanted to hug him. To feel someone, anyone, embrace her. A tear slid down her cheek as she forced her feet to stay rooted and her arms clutched about the cloak. "I shall treasure it always."

Quinn bowed again and gave her a happy nod as he stepped out into the rain ahead of her. Matthew helped her don the garment.

He pulled the large hood up to shield her head and much of her face.

"Ye need not get soaked with me, Matthew."

"He threatened ye within the kirk once before. I'll not see ye harmed because of a little rain. Besides, Quinn made me a cowl." The oiled leather hood covered him to his shoulders. "I'll be fine."

"Well, ye must come inside when we get there. I'll not have ye standing in the rain."

He inclined his head. "Ye're ever thoughtful, m'lady."

She turned as he opened the door. The rain came down in sheets that she made it impossible to see more than a step in front of her. "If I were indeed thoughtful, I'd find a place in the keep to say me prayers."

She darted down the stairs and straight for the kirk door. Head down and hood low, she didn't see him until she ran into him. Her arms whirled to regain her balance and keep her out of the mud.

There was a smack or a thud behind her. *Oof!* Matthew's legs stretched out at her feet. A hand tried to grasp her elbow but the heavy leather of her new cloak prevented him from getting a firm hold. Matthew kicked and the boots she had only seen the toes of joined Matthew on the ground.

"To the kirk, m'lady." Matthew's words were strained as he grappled with the man on the ground.

She dodged their entangled legs and started off, though she slipped and slid with the first several steps. She burst into the kirk. Brother Patrick was through his door moments later. She yelped at his appearance and clutched at her collar.

"What's happened?"

"Nathair, fights with Matthew—" She pointed as she gasped for breath.

Patrick entered his chambers for a moment, returned with a staff, and rushed past her.

When the door banged closed, she lumbered to the altar and dropped. She stared at the cross. "Why's there nowhere for me to find peace? Lord, others risk their lives for me unwanted hide. Some to save and others for evil." Her tears wet the step above where she knelt. She had no other words. Thoughts of Matthew and Patrick bloodied and dead battered her. She would never forgive herself.

The wind howled through the open door, causing Davina to jump to her feet. Her toes caught on her cloak and her gown and she fell forward before she saw who entered. Heart pounding in her ears, she didn't hear any footsteps until powerful arms pulled her to her feet. When she'd fallen, her hood had dropped forward so she didn't know who held her. She thrashed in a panic.

"Be still, m'lady. 'Tis only me."

She gasped, her arms dropped, and she leaned her head against Matthew's firm chest as the tears returned with a vengeance.

"Come now, m'lady." He eased her away and onto a pew.

She buried her face in her hands, trying to collect her rattled nerves and control herself. After a few moments, she brushed back the hood and looked at the men.

Patrick sat beside her and patted her hand. "There now, sister, all is well. No need to fret."

She looked to Matthew, who stood behind the monk, dripping mud on the tiles. A blotch peeked out from his beard on his jowl and a trickle of blood glistened on his lip. "Forgive me."

"Nay!" Matthew's rejection was so sudden and harsh she startled and the tears came again. "Ye did naught needing of forgivin'. If not even our lady can go to prayer in peace, we're in a desperate place."

Brother Patrick nodded, still patting her hand. "'Tis nigh on past time somethin' be done."

Again, Nathair disappeared from the manse, but the hall was in an uproar. Fists, tankards, and dirk hilts pounded on the boards, adding to the din of the angry voices.

Fergus sat rigid beside her.

"Forgive me for the trouble—"

His fist slammed on their table, cutting off her words. "Never, Davina. I told ye to never apologize for him." The words ground between his tight jaw as he looked out onto those gathered who had quieted at his outburst.

With slow purpose, he rose to his feet. He stretched his bent back as straight as it would go. "I hear ye and ken well yer complaints with me reprobate son, and I share them. I shall deal with him when he returns."

"Whip him!"

"Cast him out!"

"Banish him!"

The shouts bombarded around the room until Fergus raised his hand. "Aye." He quit to his cabinet, and those gathered grumbled and argued until Davina rose on quaking legs and climbed to her chamber.

She didn't come down for the midday meal. Izbeil brought her a tray later, but she had no appetite.

She curled beneath her many bedcoverings and sobbed. *Is there no home anywhere for me, Lord?*

Chapter 20

"Good gracious!"

"Brother Patrick, I'm sorry …" Davina looked up as Patrick braced himself against the wall with one hand and gulped air.

"'Tis nay yer fault, sister."

"I didn't sleep well. I'm a little late today."

The monk straightened and came to her again, laying his hand on her head as he had done the first time she came. Oh, how she craved the kind touch of another. "Almighty Father, and the Christ, watch over Yer precious daughter. Grant her the peaceful rest she needs. She's a faithful child of Yers, who comes on behalf of others. Look with Your favor upon her. Shower her with Yer mercy and grace. Protect her from all harm. In the name of Jesus, amen."

"Amen."

Patrick removed his hand, causing a chill to ripple over her. "I'll leave ye to yer intercessions."

She sat back on her heels a moment and let the prayer wash over her. She'd come today to pray for her own lonely heart. Davina brushed her aching soul aside. God did not seem inclined to provide her human comfort. Turning her mind to those within the same walls, she listed each by name and brought a request or asked for a blessing.

When she was done, she sat on a pew for a few moments, rotating her ankles and wiggling her toes. They came to life with a thousand needle pricks.

Outside, a misty fog hung so thick she couldn't see the keep. Even now, the sun only kissed the sky. At the depth of winter, there would be even fewer hours with light and warmth.

Fergus stepped out from the gray void. "Davina?"

"Good morn, m'laird." She filled her smile with warmth, hoping for the same in return.

His gaze ran the length of her. "What are ye wearin'?"

"Quinn made it to keep me dry." Her hand ran down the cloak as her fingers traced the designs.

He nodded. "Very well." No joy or approval lay in his words.

"Should I have refused it?"

"Nay, lass." He waved his hand, dismissing her concern, and continued walking. As he neared the stables, he called over his shoulder. "Matthew, I go to hunt. Guard her well."

Davina stood, rooted ankle deep in mud. The chill made her toes ache, but no water soaked them. He hadn't even greeted her. No smile. No thoughts of asking her to join him. Even tucked within the heavy leather, cold gripped her heart.

Matthew's deep voice enveloped her. "Come, m'lady. The hall fires will warm ye."

She staggered forward, sure she true warmth would evade her forever.

"Saints, m'lady!" Molly jumped and scolded her as the three maids yelped when she entered the kitchen.

Davina glanced at each concerned face. "Everyone seems on edge today."

"Has *he* returned?" Tara asked, trembling too much to continue her chopping.

Davina shook her head. "I haven't seen him. I'm sure we'll all know when he dares show his face."

"God, that he'd never return." Molly spit on the floor. "Good riddance, I say."

"Aye, that is me prayer as well," Davina said with a sigh.

"Did ye require something', m'lady?" Heather tried to change the subject.

"The laird has ridden out with some men to hunt. Ye need not set as many trays this morn."

"The man could have said sooner. Would have saved more time." Molly gave Davina a curt nod. "Will be ready with all due haste."

Davina sat at the high table alone. She was ever so tired of being alone in a crowd of people. She ate little and quit the hall to return to her chambers. Angus stopped outside as she entered. Two steps inside, as she closed the door behind her, a smell hit her. She froze. Her eyes scanned the room. Nothing looked out of place. Her heart beat against her ribs and gasping breaths brought more of the stench into her lungs. She feared she'd retch.

She backed out.

Angus drew close. "M'lady? What's wrong? Ye act as though ye've seen a spirit."

She fought to keep the terror out of her words and her voice steady. "Angus, have a few of the lads search me chamber. I think something has died in there."

Chapter 21

Davina waved Angus to follow her away from her open chamber door. Halfway down the stairs, she stopped. "I may be as rattled as the rest of the manse, but I swear Nathair was hiding in me chambers. I could smell his foul odor."

Angus hastened her down the stairs, called to Matthew, and directed her toward Fergus' cabinet. The men exchanged words at the door.

In the end, Matthew stomped away, and Angus stayed with her. "He goes to gather others to search the keep."

Davina rubbed her arms as she looked out the small window at the back of the room. The fog hadn't lifted, so she still couldn't see beyond a few feet. "He's wily. I don't expect they'll find him unless he wants them to."

"Once we've searched yer chamber and the upper floor, I'll place a guard at the top of the stairs. He'll not come back again." Angus' forced words were steeled with a hatred that tightened his fists and darkened his face.

Davina moved to the closest chair and sank into it. "Do ye think he can scale the outside and climb in me window?" She rubbed at her arms again. "I'd hate havin' to bar them as well. I'd feel like a prisoner in me own home."

"Don't ye fret, m'lady. We'll guard ye well."

"M'laird. What brings ye to me home this gloomy morn?" Quinn brushed his stained hands on his apron.

"I came to pay ye for the coat ye made Lady Davina."

"Ye will not." The tanner's arms crossed as he took a wide stance. "'Twas a gift, made for me lady. I'll not be takin' coin for it."

"It was a costly garment—in leather and time. Ye deserve—"

"Nay. I'll be takin' naught for it. Made her smile and she takes pleasure in wearin' it. 'Tis all the payment I need."

Fergus reached out his hand, but Quinn backed away, shaking his head. "Thank ye, Quinn."

"I did it for me lady."

Fergus turned his horse and joined the others who went with him for the hunt. That was becomin' the way of things in his home. He slipped into the shadows, all but forgotten, while they showered her with their love and kindness. It should have angered him, but somehow, he knew it to be right. His heart stuttered at the thought of breaking the bond they had with her.

"We found only evidence someone had waited under yer bed. He's escaped us again," Matthew said as he led the way up the stairs. They passed Grant on the last landing. The men exchanged nods. "Ye'll wait here while I check the chamber," Matthew said outside her door.

Davina leaned back against the wall and stared at the solar doors. She wished Fergus liked her enough to end their evenings there as on her first night. She sighed and let her head drop back.

"This shant last forever, m'lady. The men will find him and the laird will deal with him—if he fears his kirth and kin at all. Then, ye'll be free to come and go without fear," Grant said with a firm nod.

"Ye shall be free of Nathair's threat soon enough." Matthew stood outside her doorway. He stared at the floor, refusing to meet her gaze. He waved her inside.

She rubbed her arms. Would she never know warmth again?

The next day, as she passed Fergus on his way to his cabinet, he spoke to her without stopping. "Laird Hamish arrives this day."

"Hamish?" Matthew's sharp bark brought Fergus up short, and he turned to glare at her guard.

"Aye, Hamish." The men glared at one another until Matthew relented with a nod.

"I'll do right by ye this time, I swear," Davina mumbled in the men's silence.

Fergus sighed and continued on his way.

As she and Matthew walked to the kirk, Davina considered the exchange. "Do ye not favor this Laird Hamish?"

"Not for the business Fergus has in mind."

"I've never seen ye talk against yer laird, Matthew."

"He is me laird, and he has me fidelity, but he is wrong in this. He knows it good and well."

"Will ye stop him?"

Matthew paused and looked at her. The sadness in his eyes and voice almost brought her to tears. "If only I could, m'lady." He opened the door of the kirk and wouldn't say more.

Chapter 22

Laird Hamish had to be the biggest man Davina had ever seen. Almost a head taller than Fergus. He towered over her when Fergus brought him to the dais for introductions. But though he was tall, he was also very slender. He reminded her of an alder tree.

"Well, aren't ye just a wee lassie?"

Davina curtsied. "Welcome to our home." She kept her eyes down and her hands clasped before her.

"Very kin' of ye." Laird Hamish's voice had an odd sound to it. His words mumbled from his lips as though he spoke with several pebbles in his mouth.

They moved to the high table and, again, Fergus sat her between them. Even seated, she had to crane her neck to look at the visiting nobleman. *Thank Ye, Lord, that Crom didn't wed me to this laird. Me neck would always ache.*

"Davina, Hamish asked ye a question." Fergus' comment pulled her from her own thoughts.

She turned from Fergus to their guest. "Forgive me."

"I asked the place of yer birth, yer clan."

"Aberdeen, though I spent much time in Ansmarkt where me da

plied his trade. I'm of the Moffats." She kept her answers short. She didn't want to repeat her action of the last laird's visit. Squaring her shoulders, she glanced at Fergus in hopes her behavior would make him proud.

One corner of Fergus' mouth pulled down. Why could she not get this right?

"The Moffats of the steep or the highlands?"

"Highlands," she whispered.

So concerned with her behavior, Davina failed to eat more than a few bits. She nodded, or answered with a word or two. She wanted to please Fergus. Perhaps if she did well, he would favor her again.

When the meal concluded, Laird Hamish wiped his mouth on his sleeve. "Well, it has been an interesting meal, my ol' friend. Ye promised a respite before I returned?" Hamish pushed back from the table and stood.

"Aye, there is a room readied. Owen will show ye the way and provide anythin' ye need." Fergus' slow words leaked out heavy with resignation.

Hamish smiled at her. "Goo' sleep to ye, lassie."

Gracious, the man would never fit in one of their beds. "And to ye, m'laird." She curtsied again.

Fergus followed him out of the hall, leaving her alone. She'd failed again.

Chapter 23

Fergus was in the yard seeing Hamish on his way when Davina materialized out of the fog and headed toward the kirk. The lass still reminded him of a vision of some enchanted fairy folk, with her flaming hair and pale skin. Her ice-blue gaze caught the last of Hamish and his men melting into the mist at the gate.

Her lip slipped between her teeth for a moment before she spoke. "The laird leaves so early? Did he also refuse yer business?"

"Aye."

"'Tis for the best." Matthew blurted from behind her.

She wrung her hands. "I'm sorry, m'laird. Tell me what ye require and I'll do better."

"Davina, a lady of the manse must be hospitable."

She tipped her head, her brows pinching together. "I'm sorry. I thought …" Her hands near pulled the skin off in her fierce fidgeting, her eyes glistened with tears in the faint light, and her lip again disappeared. It was a wonder she hadn't chewed the thing off by now.

Fergus pushed a smile to his lips. "Go to yer prayers, lass. We'll talk of this later."

"Forgive me." Tears choked her words. "I'll do better. I promise I will."

"Stop thinking of me as yer da, lass. There is no punishment for you or resentment from me. We'll talk later."

"In the solar?" It was a whispered plea.

"Nay, at the meal."

She tried to stifle a whimper. "Aye, m'laird." In a few steps she was inside the kirk.

"Ye know the poor lass cries herself to sleep?" Matthew all but growled his words. He crossed his arms as he considered Fergus with a hard stare.

"Ye think me hearing goes the way of the rest of me ancient body, Matthew, that I can't hear her sobs through me door?"

"She is a fine, lass."

"Aye, and she deserves better than an ol' man the likes of me or the threat of me son."

"Ye should tell her the truth."

"I'll not discuss this with ye again." Fergus moved toward the hall.

"There'll be hell to pay later," Matthew called after him. And he was right, of course. Fergus would be in the worst hell when the dreadful matter was concluded. Lord, help him.

After several days, with no sign of Nathair and the weather clearing, the manse seemed to calm once again. Smiles returned, and the lads invited Davina to another game of shinty. The ground was soft and riddled with puddles that snagged their ball, but they laughed and it brightened her spirits.

"Here, m'lady. Pass it." Rory brushed the stick over the soggy ground, ready to move it toward the net if she hit it to him.

Wee William bounced around in his excitement. "I'm open, m'lady."

"Good hit."

It wasn't. The ball hadn't gone far and the other team had intercepted. She brushed her hand over the kind lad's head. "Thank ye, Bryce."

Oh, how the smile he gave her drove out some of the pain inside. "Davina!"

Oh, heaven help her. What had she done wrong now? "Aye, m'laird."

"Let the lads play. Come."

She sighed and handed the camen back. The boys all waved, thanked her for playing, and asked her to join them again sometime.

Fergus waited inside the door of the great hall. "This way."

"Have I done something wrong, m'laird?"

He stopped and looked at her as though she had grown another head. "Never. Why would ye say such a thing?"

"Me actions have chased off two of yer friends."

"Oh, stop frettin', Davina. Ye've done nothin' of the kind." He turned and walked across the hall. He climbed the keep steps and turned to the solar.

Maybe he wasn't mad at her. Hope flickered in her heart as he opened the door and waved her inside. But she turned when he didn't follow. "M'laird?"

He pointed to the corner.

A loom set against the wall near the window. Skeins of colorful yarn overflowed from several baskets beneath it.

The door drew closed. "Is there nothing I can do to regain yer favor?" Tears etched her words, and she hated the pleading in her voice.

He came to her. "Is that what ye think, lass? That I'm angry with ye?" He held her gaze but didn't reach out to touch her.

"Ye avoid me as if I were diseased." Her unquenchable need to be in his arms overwhelmed her. She wrapped her arms around herself as the tears flowed in unending waves.

Fergus smiled, but it didn't meet his eyes. He tipped his head. "If I hated ye, why would I buy ye a loom to occupy yer hours? Are ye not fed well and dressed in fine gowns?"

She didn't know what to say. Head down, cheeks dripping, she stepped nearer to him. *Hold me. Please, just wrap me in yer arms.*

He straightened to pull away from her. "Tell me, lass, have I not provided for ye?"

"Ye have given me all the *things* I need." He told her from her first moments in Seycoll to speak her need. Why couldn't she tell him she needed to be held?

Fergus released a satisfied sigh as he moved to the door with a dismissive flip of his hand. "Well, then. Stop yer frettin' and enjoy the warmth inside as the weather rages without."

Her thoughts tumbled until words burst forth. "Will ye stay and talk a while?"

"Nay, Nathair is still to ground. I need to meet with those who search." He closed the door behind him. She didn't make it to a chair before she crumpled in a sobbing heap.

"Ye do her wrong."

"Enough, Matthew." Fergus didn't need the reminder. This was what was best for her. He was having trouble convincing himself, though. As he charged down the stairs, Fergus opened and closed his fists several times, trying to rid them of the tension. He wanted to hold her. Fie, he loved that girl. But he knew what would be best for her. With Nathair so in disfavor with his clan, there was a new possibility for her future. He'd sent word to Malcolm and awaited his reply.

Davina did as Fergus wanted and spent much of her days locked away in the solar, weaving a new tapestry for some wall. Candles surrounded her so she could see to work, even through the short days. Storms battered the windows. Glass was expensive, and she thank the Lord for the simple blessing that allowed her to keep the shutters open to at least let her look down on her people as they scurried between buildings.

She would not labor at the loom today. Fergus met her at the bottom of the stairs and she took his arm to head to the kirk for service.

"Does the loom suit ye?"

"Aye, m'laird. Thank ye for yer kindness."

They entered in silence and exited the same after Brother Patrick concluded. She recalled little of the message.

Rory, the lad who always invited her to play, raced toward them shouting. "Luke! Has anyone seen Luke?"

Davina left Fergus' side to meet the lad. "Rory, what's the matter?"

"'Tis Mum. Fiona says she labors but the babe won't come. She sent me to find Luke." Rory leaned to look past her on the left, then the right. "Luke?" he shouted.

The physician exited the kirk at the call of his name. His gaze locked with Rory's. "I'll grab me supplies. Tell Fiona I'm comin'."

Davina draped her arm around the lad's shoulders. "Come, Rory, let's go see if we can help."

Fergus seized her elbow, pulling her up short. "And what can ye do?"

"I can sit with a frightened woman, hold her hand, and I can pray."

Fergus released her. "We shall all pray."

Davina squeezed out the cloth again and brushed it over Una's face. "Lord, mercy. We seek Ye, now. Let the bairn come. Relieve Una of this frightful pain."

Una held Davina's other hand in a fearsome grip, echoing some of the prayer. Davina re-wet the cloth and caressed it over Una's neck and collar. As the pains came, her eyes would pinch closed. When they passed, she would glance up at Davina from hooded eyes with a pleading stare.

The poor woman was beyond exhaustion when the physician at last freed the babe. Though his cry remained weak, he at least cried. As the women set about cleaning and caring for the new life and his fatigued mum, they ushered Davina out. Again, these were things *ladies* didn't do.

As her fingers slipped from Una's, the woman gripped her for a moment. "Thank ye, m'lady. I'll be there to help ye, when yer time comes."

Davina squeezed her fingers and offered her a slim smile.

She wandered from the small hut. There would be no children for her. She'd never scream in labor, nor cradle her own bairn in her arms. Her toe caught, and she stumbled. Matthew's protective arm encircled her waist before she sprawled on the ground. She turned and buried her tears in his chest.

His hands gripped her upper arms and pushed her away. "Did we lose Una?"

She shook her head, his rejection adding to her torrent of tears so she couldn't speak.

"The babe, then?"

Again, she shook her head. She jerked from Matthew's grasp and sped toward the steps. Not caring how unladylike she looked, she fled upward, through the great hall, and continued up the stairs to her chamber. Angus jumped aside as she burst into her room and slammed the door behind her.

For the next several days, she did not leave her chamber, and often dismissed Izbeil, not allowing the maid to tend her. She wouldn't dress and ate even less than when she sat beside the silent laird. Perhaps coming to Seycoll hadn't been good after all. Could she be in the loveless dungeon her father always wished for her?

"It's not right, ye pinin' up here when Una and her lad are doing so well. It isn't. Ye'll have a bairn of yer own in time. Yer jealous pouting doesn't become a lady. It doesn't." Izbeil didn't understand. No one did.

Davina yanked the covers over her head to drown out Izbeil's chastisement. The maid was right, of course. But Davina couldn't bear to hear the words.

After two days of bright sun shining in her room, she went across the hall and sat at her loom.

"Ye must come down to the hall, m'lady. The laird asks after ye. He does."

"Fergus doesn't give a wit if I'm there or not," she spat.

Izbeil gasped, "M'lady!"

"How many days have I remained abed? He's not once come to see for himself how I faired."

"The laird cares for ye more than ye know, m'lady." Matthew stood in the open doorway, holding her in a disapproving stare.

Izbeil nodded as she glanced between Davina and Matthew. Her brows pinched. "Aye. He's asked many times after ye. He does."

Davina looked between the two. They sounded so earnest of Fergus' concern and care. She pushed to her feet and lumbered down the stairs.

Fergus stood when he saw her, a near smile on his face. He gripped her hand and held it in a fierce grasp. "Oh, it does me heart good to see ye, lass."

"Does it?"

He squeezed her hand again. "We've all missed ye, Davina." He drew her attention to those gathered at the boards. They'd stopped eating or talking to look at her. Every face filled with a smile. She inclined her head as they called out a shout of welcome.

Maybe they wanted her here after all.

Chapter 24

After a week at her loom, the frame sat strung, and she'd completed two finger's width of the pattern. The vertical frame was large enough to create a tapestry that could cover her bed. It could take a year to finish. She sighed and glanced out the windows.

The sun struggled through the late morning fog. Midday would be soon. Maybe the lads would be playing after the meal and she could get out of these walls and be with others.

"M'lady?" She turned at the voice she didn't recognize right away. Owen stood beside her guard. "The laird requested ye come to the cabinet."

She glanced at Matthew, who nodded his approval. She secured her bobbins and stretched her tight muscles. Descending the stairs before both men, she turned and raised her hand to knock. Owen opened it before she could and ushered her inside. Fergus was not within.

"The laird wished me to teach ye to read," Owen said as he indicated a chair for her.

Davina stared at him. The words would not take root in her addled brain. "Read?"

"Aye." Owen smiled and waved again at Fergus' chair behind the desk. "A lady should have the ability to read, so she can better tend to the needs of the day to day running of the manse."

"I thought ye took care of these matters and the laird oversaw yer work."

"'Tis just as important for the lady in conscripting works for the kitchens and record keeping. Do ye not wish to learn?"

"Saints alive, yes. I have wanted to read for as long as I can remember. Crom never saw the point of educating a female."

"Laird Fergus values education and encourages any who wish to better themselves. Shall we begin?"

Davina nodded and sat as Owen picked up a framed bit of slate and hunk of chalk. "Words are composed of letters," he said. Taking the chalk, he drew each one and said its name as she watched.

When he finished, she slid to the edge of her seat. "Repeat them, please."

He pointed to each one, saying its name.

"Okay, how do they form words?"

"M'lady, ye go too fast. First, ye must learn and remember the letters."

"I have."

"M'lady …"

She reached for the slate. With a bit of cloth, she rubbed it clean and took the chalk from him. "Which letter do ye wish?"

He looked at her with a raise brow. "C."

She drew it and showed him.

Both brows now rose as he said another. He continued. "X. M. E."

She drew each until she had written them all. Then, she cleaned the slate and wrote them all in the order he had to begin with, saying each as she did.

"By my sword, ye know them."

She considered him. "Was that not what ye wished?"

"Aye, but it can take a week or better for most to learn what ye just did in an hour."

Davina looked at the slate, her heartbeat stuttered. "Will it make the laird proud?"

"M'lady, he is already proud. There is nothin' ye can do to make him favor ye more."

She dared to raise her head and look at him. There was the same sadness in his eyes she often noticed in Matthew's. But his smile was genuine, and it gave her courage to move forward. "So, how do these form words?"

"The meal is ready." They both looked up at Matthew's head poking in the open door.

"We will save that for the morrow after the morning meal." Owen bowed.

Davina didn't want to stop, but she took her place beside Fergus as he filled her plate. "Thank ye, m'laird." He paused considering her. "For the reading lessons. I've always wanted to learn."

He smiled. "It is me pleasure to find something to brighten yer day, lass."

"Ugh!" Davina pushed back her chair and stomped to the window.

"Ye're makin' fine progress, m'lady."

"A sennight of fighting with the unruly letters and I show little mastery of recognizing them in words."

"Ye expect too much of yerself," Owen muttered.

"I learned all the names of those in the manse in a day. These confounding letters in an hour. Why do words frustrate me so?"

Owen paused for a moment before he explained. "A man's name is his name from birth. A letter is always a letter."

"But when ye put the wee letters together, they are not always the same," she said with a sigh

"Aye!"

Davina stomped her foot. "Sometimes they make one sound and other times something completely different." She stalked to Fergus' bookshelf and yanked a fat volume down. Dropping it on the desk with a thud, she opened it to a random page and tried to read several words.

Owen scooped it up. "Perhaps, m'lady, ye should start with somethin' a little more interestin' than the annual reports of the manse." He replaced the volume and pulled another slimmer one from further down the wall. "This is a grand adventure of love and honor."

She opened it to the first page and tried. Owen gave her the words she floundered over. It took several minutes, but she finished the first page. The story made more sense than the single words she'd been practicing. The next page came easier.

Within another sennight, she'd finished the entire book and needed less and less of Owen's help. "May I choose another?"

Owen grinned. "The laird has said ye may read them all, if it pleases ye, m'lady."

"Would ye recommend another?"

Owen drew one and then pointed out others she might enjoy. She took it to her room and read a little by candlelight each night. Between the morning lessons, afternoons at the loom and evenings alone with a book, she spent less with those who shared her home. The weather churned outside as winter dragged on. Even under Crom's roof, she had never been so alone.

Chapter 25

The wind howled and buffeted against the walls as Davina moved from the cabinet where she'd been reading Scripture with Patrick to the meal. Fergus stood and greeted her. He smiled, as he always did, but they hadn't said more than a handful of words to each other in weeks.

Fergus filled her plate. "That's plenty, m'laird."

"Ye aren't eatin' enough, lass."

She pulled the plate toward her and chased the food around, nibbling now and then.

Boom! The outer doors burst open with a gale of wind, sending reeds into the air and plaid whipping about. A moment later, everything stilled and quieted, but standing inside the now closed doors were four soaked men. They shook themselves off and wrung their plaids. A younger man in the back removed a boot and upturned it to dump the water within on the floor.

"Malcolm." Fergus stood with an excited call and made his way to the older man in the front of the group. His full bushy beard and dark curly hair were beginning to gray. Malcolm might be two score older than Davina and broader in shoulder than Fergus.

The two men greeted one another with a mighty embrace. They

exchanged words before they returned to the dais. "Laird Malcolm, this is the Lady Davina."

The laird's smile, though it remained hidden with the mass of hair on his face, brightened his eyes as he bowed deep at the waist. "It be me pleasure to make yer acquaintance."

Be hospitable. Be hospitable. She took a slow, steadying breath as she curtsied. "Might we offer ye some dry clothes and a proper meal?"

"Oh, ye're kind, m'lady." His hand waved out toward the large fire at the back of the hall where his men stood. "A few moments at yer hearth and I shall be dry enough to enjoy good food and fine fellowship with friends new …" His head inclined toward her. "… and old." He bobbed a nod at Fergus.

When the visiting laird moved to the fire, Davina slipped into the kitchen for another plate and cup.

"I'll bring them out straight away, m'lady," Heather said.

"Oh, by the saints, I am not too delicate to carry one set of dishes." She thrust her arms forward and snatched the items before any of them could protest.

There was a bit of a stomp in her steps when she reentered the hall. Fergus and Matthew both stared at her. Davina stopped and took a deep breath before she proceeded with more calm. Malcolm joined her as Fergus took the items from her and sat them to her right.

Be hospitable. Be hospitable. She would not shame Fergus again. She would get this right.

Fergus passed Malcolm the tray of food as they all sat.

She left her small portion untouched. "What brings ye out in such foul weather, m'laird?"

"I had important business in Ansmarkt that couldn't wait. And Fergus asked me to be sure and pay him a visit the next I passed this way. He told of a treasure in his home I must see with me own eyes. Had I known the jewel who would greet me, I would have come far sooner."

He gave a slight nod and winked at her as he filled his mouth with roast boar.

"Thank ye. Ye be too kind." Heat seared her cheeks, but his twinkling eyes left her wanting to smile back at him. "I pray the storm relents before ye must leave."

"I welcome time with clan Fullarton. They are good people."

Her gaze swept out over the hall. "Aye, m'laird. They are the finest."

He mumbled his agreement as he continued to clear his plate as though he hadn't eaten in days. "How have ye passed these stormy days?"

She glanced at Fergus, who encouraged her to respond with a raise of his chin. "Laird Fergus has provided me a wall loom and access to his library."

"As I remember, Fergus has a great deal of fine volumes. Do ye read in Gaelic or Latin?

"I do better in Gaelic though me Latin is improving."

"What have ye found of interest?"

Davina settled into the amiable conversation with an eagerness that surprised her. "There are several French romances that the first Fullarton lady favored. They were translated into Latin and I am using them to acquire the language better."

"Aye, the lassies love the romances. Have ye read any of the ancient tomes? I hear tell Alistair Douglas transcribed Virgil's Aeneid."

Davina chuckled. "I have only just started exploring the library, m'laird. It may be some time before I get to every book."

"Aye and there is the creation on the loom and the running of the manse, which must necessitate many hours of yer day."

She liked this laird. He was quiet and agreeable. He sipped from his cup and wiped his mouth on his sleeve. "Fergus, what say we retire to the warmth of yer solar and share of events since last we saw each other?"

Fergus stood and put out his arm for Davina. She was startled that he wished to include her.

"As ye are by far the biggest news, Ol' Fergus has to share, ye must come, m'lady." She turned to see Malcolm leaning near her shoulder. His eyes danced with merriment.

Davina led the way up the narrow stairs. Had she left the solar in good order? No one used it but her. Was her yarn strewn about? Where the candles melted nubs? Her hands clenched tighter on the fist-fulls of fabric she held to keep from tripping as she climbed.

She sighed at the tidy room and slipped into a chair near the fire while Fergus filled their cups.

She sipped on the sour ale. The berry mead she favored had run out a few weeks ago. Fergus and Molly promised her many barrels as soon as the fruit ripened again.

Laird Malcom took the drink Fergus offered and continued to her loom. "A fine hand, Lady Davina." His voice smiled, even though she couldn't see his face. "Might it be a scene from one of your romances?"

She met his wide grin with a smirk. "I hoped to depict David's victory over the giant Goliath."

Malcolm lowered into the seat to her right. "Trusting God as we battle our giants and trials." He nodded and sipped his drink. "Always an excellent lesson." He considered her with a long stare. "I pray your life, dear lady, has not seen many trials."

Tears stung her eyes, and she blinked them away as she stared into her near full cup. "In this life ye shall know trials …"

"But take heart, for I have overcome the world." Malcolm raised his cup to her when she glanced up. A grin greeted her, too. "The Lord promised to fight for His children."

She nodded, unable to contain the delight bubbling in her. She relaxed into her chair as their conversation continued with ease.

"Excuse me m'lairds, m'lady, the evenin' meal is ready." Matthew drew their attention.

"So soon?" Davina had been so engrossed in the lively conversation, she'd not noticed how much time had passed.

"'Tis been a delight, sharin' the afternoon with ye, m'lady." Malcolm extended his hand and pulled her to her feet before he bowed.

"I have enjoyed it as well, m'laird."

A look passed between Fergus and Malcolm. She'd forgotten Fergus was there as he'd said very little as Malcolm asked her questions and plied her with funny tales. The glance lasted but a moment, but they both smiled and then turned their bright faces to her. It seemed clear she had not chased this laird away as she'd done the others. Why, then, did her stomach twist in knots and her mouth go dry?

Chapter 26

"I thought we'd begin practice with some numbers today." Owen greeted Davina at the bottom of the stairs the next morning.

"What of breaking the fast with Laird Malcolm?"

Owen directed her toward the cabinet with a wave of his hand. "The storm broke, so he and his men rode for Ansmarkt early. He will stop again on his return." An odd catch pitched the tenor of his words.

"Has he agreed to Fergus' business?"

Owen turned away from her. "Aye." The word was quiet and full of dread.

"Is it not good, sir?"

Owen's shoulders slumped. "'Tis for the best," he mumbled with a sigh.

Again, Davina struggled to swallow, trying to shake the wave of fear and unease washing over her like last night's storm. "I'll go to prayers, if the storm has broken, and return soon."

"As ye wish, m'lady."

As she rested on her knees before the altar, words wouldn't come. She'd done well and even enjoyed herself with the visiting laird. Fergus had seemed pleased. But the memory of the exchanged glance between the lairds, the miserable look in Owen's and Matthew's eyes, and the despondency when they spoke prevented her heart from a sure beat.

"Lord …" Her plea died. Why was she so fearful? What did they know that she didn't?

"Lord, I …"

She drew in a deep breath and let her head bow low. "I trust in Ye and Yer care for me. Ye are ever a good Father." Her next breath came with ease. At last, she turned her concerns to her kirth and their needs.

For several days, Owen taught her numbers and how to complete simple calculations on the slate. Though she could count and do simple figures in her head, this was the first time anyone taught her what those figures looked like when written.

Another Lord's Day came. Fergus stooped so now he was shorter than her. His feet shuffled in the mud. It was as if he'd aged a handful of years just since Laird Malcolm had visited.

Davina clung tighter to his arm. "Are ye hale, m'laird?"

His watery gaze held hers as he forced his lips to draw up in a half smile that touched no other part of his features. "As well as I might be, lass." He patted her hand where it rested on his arm. Again, they ate in silence. And now Fergus ate as little as she did.

Matthew stared at the floor and never touched the food passing up and down the board in front of him. Owen also ate little, and a weight fell over Davina that chilled her entire frame. Something was very wrong. What had she done?

Davina stared out the dark window. Would winter ever end? It covered the land as a darkness consumed her spirit.

Izbeil finished straightening her room. "Do ye not wish to go to yer prayers today, m'lady?"

Was she avoiding God? No matter the turmoil in Crom's home, her God had never failed. Without Him, what hope was there? In His presence was the only place she'd find her answers and comfort.

She turned without a word and lumbered to the door.

"Chin up, m'lady. Ye'll have bairns soon enough. All is in the Good Lord's hands. We should not doubt His timing."

Davina fled the room without a word to her well-meaning maid. Matthew kept pace with her as she raced down the stairs, but even he spoke little now.

The chill within the kirk was even more biting than the wind outside. Perhaps it was not her surroundings but something within herself. The defect had to be in her, for the Lord of all was perfect.

She knelt, unable to pray as tears wet her lap.

Though Owen grew near as quiet as Fergus and Matthew, he still insisted she come and learn each morning following her prayers. Her supplications seemed to fall on a God as distant and aloof as the men surrounding her.

Owen sat an odd shaped book in front of her. "This is a ledger. In it, we record all the purchases for the running of the manse and all the income we receive from our fiefs."

Davina scanned the neat lines of items followed by a column of numbers on the other side of the page. "Sir, does this not say beets?"

He glanced where her finger pointed. "Aye?"

"Does this mean we purchase beets at the market for our kitchens?"

He straightened with a satisfied nod. "That is exactly what it means."

"Excuse me, one mite, sir." She slipped from the room and made her way to the kitchens. "Molly?"

"Aye." The cook continued her work with but a brief glance her direction.

"Do we have beets in our stores?"

The cook had her hands full of hunks of meat and pointed with her elbow. "They sit in the bottom of the larder, till they rot. Then, they're replaced by a fresh bag."

Davina closed her eyes and tried to remember all the meals she'd had since she'd arrived. "But ye don't use them in any of the dishes ye serve do ye?"

Molly finished adding her meat to the large pot hanging over a low fire. "By the sword, no!" Her nose crinkled and her lips twisted. "Nasty things. Can't stand 'em."

"Lady Sile favored them," Heather said, wiping her hands on her apron. "No one else in the entire manse like the bloody root."

Davina looked around the room at the women. "Then why, by the saints, do we still purchase them?"

They shrugged, and Davina returned to the cabinet. "I don't understand the figures these numbers represent, sir, but Molly assures me she never cooks with beets and the things always go to rot. We need not purchase them again."

Owen's shoulders squared, and his mouth drew in a harsh line.

Davina plopped in the chair with a groan. "I've spoken out of turn again. I didn't mean to offend, sir."

He shook his head. "Nay, m'lady. Ye've already seen where we might save a little coin. Well done, m'lady." His kind words didn't match his countenance.

Davina took his words to be true and scanned the list of items further. Owen guided her down each page.

She burst from the chair a short time later, almost colliding with the man leaning over her shoulder. "Venison?"

Owen leaned back with his face crunched. "Aye?"

Again, she went to the kitchen. Owen shadowed her this time through the near empty hall. "Molly, another question."

The cook huffed, but looked toward Davina. "Ye're busy today, m'lady."

"Owen is showing me the ledger. Do our men not hunt enough meat to fulfill our needs?"

As if explaining matters to a young child, Molly nodded and plodded through her words. "We have fine hunters, m'lady."

"Aye," Heather and Tara said as one.

Davina glanced at Owen. "Then there would never be a need to purchase meat."

The backs of Molly's mired hand perched on her hips. "Never!"

Davina nodded and turned with another look at Owen as she moved to leave the kitchen. "Thank ye."

Back in Fergus' cabinet, she looked at the steward. "Owen, how much has been spent on venison?"

The man scanned the records. "About a bonnet a year."

Davina dropped into the chair. "Is that not close to forty shillings?"

"Aye, what is the matter?"

"You heard it yerself, sir. We need no venison. Our men hunt ample meat for all the people of Seycoll."

The color drained from Owen's face.

"Who makes these purchases?" She feared she already knew the answer.

Owen shook his head as he paced and muttered under his breath.

After the third circuit, Davina sagged back in her chair. "Nathair."

Owen stopped in mid-stride. "I'll inform the Laird of what ye've uncovered. Will break his heart."

A spark of hope flared within her. Could this be their answer? "But he sought a way to bring charges against Nathair?"

"M'lady, regardless of what the ne'er-do-well has done, the laird loves him and hates to bring him harm. Even when 'tis the honorable thing to do."

At the meal, she wanted to tell Fergus as it was the only time she ever saw him, but he did not join her. Matthew didn't seem to know where he was either. She ate alone. Well, she stirred her food around her plate, unable to even force more down her tight throat.

Davina returned after the meal to practice simple calculations on the slate, but a shift in the lesson's mood left her aching for a time when Nathair's behavior no longer overshadowed every corner of the manse. He had wrought such evil as his da looked the other way, hoping he would transform into a man of honor.

Chapter 27

Davina left her loom and descended the stairs for midday, though she didn't see the point of sitting next to a man who wouldn't speak to her. Neither of them ate much and whatever was amiss between them now seemed to affect the entire hall. From the muted laughter to the sparse whispered conversation, it hurt to breathe in a room so stifled.

As she rounded the corner and stepped up onto the dais, Nathair leapt up on the other end of the long, raised platform. They stood still, staring at one another. Only about half the room had gathered, but one could have heard a thimble drop in the rushes.

She fingered the dirk hidden in the folds of her skirt. Nathair had been gone so long, she'd forgotten to wear it a few times. The leather against her fingers gave her strength to step toward her place.

"Nathair." She didn't smile or incline her head only acknowledged his presence.

"Woman." The word spit from his lips.

Two thumping steps behind her told her that Matthew dared climb the dais. He would intervene if need be. But she had no mind to give Nathair any ground in their struggle. She took another purposeful step toward her seat.

She kept her gaze on him. "Ye should let the kitchen know ye'll be here for the meal. Has been long, and they no longer set a place for ye."

"Ye'll not be rid of me with such ease, wench." The words were deep and menacing.

"I'm the lady of the manse, Nathair, and ye'll address me as my station demands." She prayed her words didn't tremble as the rest of her body. Her fingers tightened around the dirk.

"'Tis me home and I'll treat ye as I see fit. But it matters not, as I've only come to collect the coin for the month's purchases."

She should have kept her mouth closed and let Fergus deal with him, but the words burst forth of their own. "Ye'll not receive good coin for beets no one eats and the manse coffers will never again pay for meat we don't need and never take possession of." The bold statement had erupted from her lips far too loud.

Muttering filled the hall as more gathered.

"Ye wretched whore!" Nathair lunged at her, hand raised to strike.

A roar exploded behind her.

The polished silver of her small blade streaked through the air. It sliced across Nathair's palm. He jerked away. She held the dirk extended before her, the blood-drenched tip pointed at him, ready in case he struck again.

"Nathair!" Fergus stood at her left. "How dare ye—"

"How dare I! How dare ye brin' this common trollop into me home. She's younger than I and ye only bed her to replace me. I'll not allow ye to sweep me aside as ye do the filthy rushes on the flore. In fact …" Nathair snatched up a feasting knife from beside his father's plate. "I'll take me inheritance now—and whatever else I please."

Nathair thrust the single-edged blade at his father. Davina sidestepped in between them. The knife pierced her side. Bolts of pain rippled through her body.

"Davina!" Fergus grabbed hold of her and held her steady.

"M'lady!" The cries echoed through the room, but none was louder than Matthew as he tried to push past them on the narrow platform.

Davina took hold of Matthew's arm, stopping him. Pushing aside the pain, she drew air into her lungs and forced it out with a loud shout. "Ye heard him. Ye can all bear witness. This man is a disgrace of the worse kind. He tried to murder his own father."

"Aye!" those in the hall roared until the dinnerware rattled.

The hatred in Nathair's eyes flickered with fear.

"Ye saw him. He intended this knife …" She pointed to the short blade penetrating her side, just above her hip. "… for his own father."

"Aye!"

"He has broken faith with his liege laird," she continued.

"Aye!" Now they not only shouted, but men of the manse moved forward.

"And worse, with his own blood." Davina fought for breath. Her legs quaked. The room swayed.

"Aye! 'Tis treason!" The men neared the dais to cut off his retreat.

"God's law states, 'Also he that smiteth his father or his mother, shall die the death.'" Brother Patrick shouted above the other voices.

"Aye, he deserves death!" The women and children still at the tables pounded on them. Men moved ever closer to Nathair. Matthew broke free of her weakening grasp.

She glanced at the blood flowing down her skirt and her knees buckled.

Fergus eased her to the floor as Nathair leapt from the dais, fled the angry men, and crashed through the kitchen door.

"I'm here, m'lady. Ye'll be ta right again, I swear it." Luke's face blurred as the physician came to kneel beside her.

Fergus stroked her face. "Oh, lass. Forgive me."

Chapter 28

Davina woke with a scream as fire seared her side. Firm hands held her legs and shoulders to keep her from thrashing.

"Peace, m'lady. Will be over soon. It will." Izbeil brushed her face with a damp cloth, but that wasn't where she burned.

They pitched her to her right side and another intolerable pain burst through her, tearing free another scream.

"Oh, lass. I'm so sorry." Fergus was here. In her chamber. What of Nathair? Would things be different between her and the indifferent laird now? More pain and prodding drove out any other thought.

"Lass, forgive me yet again, but ye need to wake." A rough, gnarled hand caressed her face.

Were her lids sewn shut? One at last pried open. A blurry form sat on her bed. Someone had drawn all the bed-curtains to reveal two more forms standing nearby. By the shape of one, she knew Izbeil paced at the end of the bed.

"The time has come, my precious lass." Fergus's trembling hand stroked hers.

Was she dying? Davina's vision cleared. Tears welled in Fergus' eyes and Izbeil's cheeks were damp. Even Duncan looked to be crying. Why was Duncan in her chamber?

"Fergus?" Her voice was brittle, strained by her parched throat.

After lifting her head and helping her drink, Fergus patted her hand. "Now, don't ye fret, lass. Duncan'll take good care of ye. He'll see ye arrive safe."

She couldn't breathe. As though the entire keep collapsed upon her, she fought to draw air into her chest. She grasped at Fergus' tunic, but he held her hand. "Please, I'll be good. I'll do whatever ye ask. I shall never come out of the solar if ye wish. Please, m'laird."

His head hung and shook. "Nay, lass 'tis not a punishment. 'Tis for ye best, ye'll see. Laird Malcolm was to collect ye when he returned, but ye're not safe here now, Davina."

Again, she fought to seize hold of him, but she was too weak. "Please, m'laird."

Fergus cleared his throat, trying to sound stern, but the words came out a moan. "Now lass, 'tis for the best. Malcolm has agreed to yer marriage to his son Callen."

"No! I'm yer wife. M'laird, please, whatever ye require I'll do it." Her words croaked through her sobs.

"I wish ye to know love. To cradle yer bairns to yer bosom. To raise fine, honorable lads, and sweet bonny lasses. Do this for me, Davina."

She tossed her head, struggling to rise. "Nay, I'm yer wife."

"Lass, I'm sorry, but yer not."

"But we said the words at the door of the kirk."

"I said some words, but never said wife. I promised only to look after ye and I have."

"Crom signed an agreement for marriage."

"The man couldn't read. He signed ye over as me ward, lass. I swore to save ye from the evil he aimed to inflict on ye and do what he refused to do . I found ye a good match, Davina. Callen is a fine lad."

"But I was the lady of the manse." Her tear-filled words pleaded as she struggled to reach for him again.

"Aye, lass. Ye are the finest of us."

"Please, don't send me away." Her word stuttered through her growing sobs.

"'Tis not safe. Nathair escaped, vowing vengeance on ye and some within these walls helped him, m'lady." Duncan's voice sputtered through his tears, too.

"But I'm not *yer* lady, now, am I?" Bitterness cracked like a whip through the air and, though she spoke to the kind-hearted man, her angry gaze never left Fergus'.

Duncan straightened and his words surged out like waves in a storm. "Ye are now, and ever shall be, me lady."

Davina softened and pleaded with Fergus yet again. "Please." It was the only word she could manage.

"I've known from the moment I saw ye, me bonny lass, it'd break me heart to send ye away. But I can't give ye what ye need and ye'll never be safe here with Nathair and his ilk lurkin' about." Fergus staggered to his feet and turned toward his door. "I've loved ye like a daughter and I shall go to me grave knowin' I caused ye nothin' but pain."

"What if I refuse to leave? Scream and thrash so ye can't carry me away?"

Duncan answered. "Then, to the man—"

"—and woman." Izbeil added.

"—we'll die to protect ye. Every one of us will stand between ye and any who dare do ye harm, m'lady," Duncan swore.

Fergus was gone when she looked back. She gave up the fight. Every muscle fell lax, as sobs racked her body.

"Now, come, m'lady, we need to dress ye for the journey. The storm has passed but the air will chill you to the bone. It will. Duncan, love, step out. I'll call ye when she's ready."

She did nothing to assist Izbeil in changing her gown or donning her heavy leather coat and boots.

"Come, now, m'lady. Laird Callen is a fine lad. Seen him many times when he and his da passed through Seycoll. He is fine in form and manners. He is."

Seycoll. Her home. Or so she thought. But Fergus didn't want her here. He'd lied and betrayed her. He sent her to another man's arms. This was worse than what Crom had done.

She didn't remember Duncan entering the room or scooping her up, but she lay cradled against his chest. "Ye'll need to be quiet, m'lady. The conspirators can't know yer leavin' the manse."

She wanted to scream to the heavens. To kick and writhe in his arms. But it would serve no purpose. Davina filled one hand with Duncan's tunic and buried her tears in his chest.

CHAPTER 29

Wispy clouds played hide-and-peek with the waning moon as Izbeil led the way across the bit of grass where she had played with the lads. Davina would never see them again. She was forbidden to bid farewell to any of those who had so knit themselves into her heart.

Duncan's shirt would not contain her tears as they neared the back wall. "Shh, 'tis only a little farther."

They slipped around a large boulder, leaning against the seawall. Hidden within its deep shadows was a metal door. Izbeil unlocked it and stepped inside. They stood in utter blackness until a flame flickered and brought a torch to life.

As Izbeil continued ahead of them, Duncan twisted and turned to squeeze along the narrow passage and down winding stairs, carrying Davina in his arms.

Let the dark take her. What did it matter now? Better to come to her end here than be forced to leave the only place she thought of as home. But Duncan never stopped, determined to see her delivered to be yet another man's wife.

Waves echoed against the stonewalls as they descended. Izbeil soon stepped into a small skiff and Duncan lay Davina down at his wife's feet. He untied the rope from its moorings and stepped in, making the small craft pitch deep on one side. Oh, that it would hurl her over the side and let the waves swallow her.

Duncan took up the oars and propelled them toward a small opening trimmed in pale moonlight. The torch hissed out in the sea. A few strokes outside the opening, Davina turned back to see her beloved Seycoll for one last time. The sheer cliffs topped with mighty walls glistened in the silvery light, and they stood strong and unaffected by her leaving. When she could no longer make out any sign of her near island, Davina buried her face in Izbeil's lap and sobbed until sleep claimed her.

As she drifted between asleep and awake, bobbing in the small craft, heat warmed her. Later, the wind bit at her flesh as the warmth and light slipped away. Izbeil forced her to drink, but she refused to eat.

"Now, m'lady, ye need to regain yer strength. Ye must eat. Ye must." Izbeil stroked her shoulder.

The tears started again and Davina hid her face in the maid's skirts.

Izbeil's hand smoothed her hair. "Oh, m'lady, 'tis not as bad as all that. Ye'll be happy with Laird Callen. Ye'll will."

"I want to go home," Davina muttered.

"Ye are goin' home, m'lady," Duncan's rhythm never slowed, but his words dragged with sadness.

She slept more than she was awake. How long had they been on the boat? Davina wanted to stretch her stiff muscles. The cycle of fiery glare and chilly darkness led her to believe days had passed. Each moment had taken her farther away from the place and people most dear to her.

They lurched forward as the skiff scraped against sand. Davina woke and shivered in the night air. Duncan stepped out, held the craft still for his wife, and then she held it as Duncan scooped Davina up again. She whimpered as throbbing pain spread through her middle.

"Forgive me."

She buried her face against Duncan's shoulder, but cried out as he worked to hold her more securely.

"Is that ye, Duncan?" a voice called out of the darkness.

Every muscle in Duncan's body stiffened. "Who's there?" He turned, searching the dark strip of sand beside them and then the rise above.

"Ewan. Fergus sent me to assist ye."

Davina tried to recall the name in the haze of pain. Ewan? Did she remember him? A man about the age of Nathair. Were the two friendly?

"Nay, the laird didn't, love," Izbeil whispered to her husband as she leaned against them both.

"Ewan, have ye horses to carry our lady to the Laird Macay?"

"Aye, we can be there before sunrise. Hand the lady up and I'll prepare to take her straight away." The shadow, near ten feet above them, leaned out over the edge.

Laird Malcolm was of clan Kincaid. Duncan told a lie to determine if this Ewan was friend or another enemy.

Davina shuttered. Would she find safety anywhere in the entire country?

Duncan glance to Izbeil with a nod as he called up to Ewan. "I haven't the strength, lad. Been rowing all day and night. We'll come around."

"Fine." The word was spit in disgust. Pebble sprinkled down the rock face as Ewan moved away from the edge.

Duncan turned and started down the narrow beach toward the rocky ridge where Ewan waited above. He walked with Izbeil behind him until he came to an overhang where he stepped out of Ewan's sight. He sat Davina against a large rock and Izbeil supported her.

"Does our lady still have her dirk?" Duncan whispered.

"Nay," Izbeil shook her head. "I think it remained in the hall when she collapsed."

Duncan snatched up Davina's satchel of gowns and his wife's cloak and made a bundle that looked like a body. With the unruly cloth in his arms and his sword in his hand, he prepared to continue.

"Where are ye, man?" Ewan called.

"As I said, has been a long journey, and I'm not the spry youth I once was." Duncan returned to the path and staggered out of sight of the women.

Izbeil tightened her grip around Davina as the crunching of sand under his feet faded. A long, unbearable silence followed.

"Lord, guard Duncan," Davina whispered. Her head slumped to Izbeil's shoulder. Sleep was all she wanted. Sleep and to have Duncan return safe. And to go home.

Izbeil stroked Davina's arm. "Me Duncan is well skilled with the sword. He is. He'll be fine. Just fine."

Did she try to assure Davina or herself?

The clash of metal broke the quiet, startling them both.

Chapter 30

The sword fight between Duncan and Ewan was quick. But who survived? Heavy steps approached the quaking women at last. Izbeil moved to stand between the coming victor and Davina.

"Please, Lord," Davina mumbled. She may want it all to end for her, but she couldn't bear for anything to happen to Izbeil and her beloved Duncan.

"Ah, me love, ye dispatched the villain. Ye did."

"Swiftly." Duncan eased Davina into his arms again. "We've gained his horse. Will make the journey quicker, though less comfortable with yer injury, I fear."

Up on the rise, Duncan placed Davina in the saddle and Izbeil sat behind her to hold her steady. Both Duncan and her maid held her, but it was in order to steal her from her home. This is not the type of touch she wanted. The journey, leaving her beloved Seycoll, and her injuries conspired to pull her into sleep. Her head lulled in every direction as she fought to stay awake.

Duncan led them as fast as he could run, but he was tired too.

The ocean waves still called to her when Duncan drew them up short and his sword sang from the sheath. Davina struggled to keep her eyes open to notice what new danger they faced. Passing Izbeil the reins, he moved toward two horses standing in the shadows.

When next Davina woke, Duncan had pulled her from one saddle to cradle her where he sat astride another. Izbeil remained on the horse they'd shared and led a third horse draped with two bodies covered with their plaids.

"Who—?" Davina muttered. There was no moon to give them light, but the sky was alive with stars.

Duncan drew her leather cloak around her as she shivered. "A Kincaid and a Frazer's man."

Her thoughts muddled, was there a sword fight? Two? "Did they attack us too?"

"Nay, m'lady. They were already dead when we came upon their horses."

Davina let go of the reasons and the potential killer. Every part of her body now ached.

The horses plodded over soft turf that made little noise. Night insects calling in the distance, quieted when they neared and resumed their chatter when they passed. The jarring of her body was the only other thing to mark the time passing.

She wanted to be still and forget everything in the oblivion of sleep's embrace—and then never wake. But he spurred the horse to speed, and they bounded as fast as Duncan dared in the weak light.

A voice captured her attention. "Who goes there?" Light leaked into the eastern sky behind forms on horses.

Duncan reined in hard, jarring her aching body. "Who wants to know?" Duncan fought to get hold of his sword with Davina sprawled across his lap.

"Laird Malcolm's men."

Duncan's muscles tensed. "Can ye prove that?"

"He returned to Seycoll to collect a treasured gift Laird Fergus had given him. But for safety, Fergus had sent the prize on ahead. Laird Malcolm raced home to receive this precious gem, but it had yet to arrive. Now, who goes there?"

What were these shadows talking about? There faint images blurred together so Davina couldn't tell who stood in their path.

"Duncan of the Fullarton. I bring the gift he seeks."

He did? What gift—her? They were talking about her as a jewel and a gift. Why did that only make her want to cry again?

The two groups approached one another, swords still in hand, and reins held tight.

"Boyd, 'tis good to see ye. We've met those seeking the lady further harm and we bring yer dead," Duncan said.

"Come, let's make haste before any other graves need be dug."

Sounds echoed around her and came in spirts as she slipped between awareness and the void. The thundering of the hooves filled air devoid of any hint of salt. Strong winds rang empty of any waves. The jarring of the galloping horse made sleep impossible. All hope lost. Davina didn't even have any more tears to cry.

"Open the gates." Flames flickered along the wall and the hinges protested as they sped past. "Wake the healer."

"I'll take her," someone offered.

"Nay, I'll assure m'lady safety and deliver her to her chambers." Duncan dismounted while his still held her. Though, his arms now trembled.

They passed through a small dim hall and up the stairs of the keep. Sleep beckoned, but not before they passed a room bright with light peeking around the near-closed door.

"Father, I'll not discuss this further. Ye can't force me to marry her. I'm not Dougal who ye bend to yer every whim. I'm tellin' ye, I don't want her! Send her back."

Chapter 31

Davina feigned sleep as many hands worked to redress her wound. Even cauterizing it hadn't prevented the bleeding from returning in the rough escape from Nathair's threat.

"Oh, she's a bonny lass, this one. Laird Callen will be pleased," a woman's voice giggled.

"He rails at his father's arrangement, but one look at the lady and he'll be eating his refusal." A different, older voice assured.

The maids laughed, unaware that she had listened for a short time. She'd not force the man to marry. She'd not stay where she wasn't wanted. Never again. Sleep. She found a sanctuary from her despair in its dark embrace.

"Izbeil?"

"Yer maid has left, m'lady." A cup pressed against her lips and a cold liquid slipped into her mouth. "To keep yer whereabouts from being discovered, the laird thought it best they moved away from here with all haste. I'm Morag. I'm here to serve ye."

Davina turned away as the tears started again. Her dear maid was just one more in a long list of beloved souls they robbed her of the chance to bid farewell. Thankfully, sleep claimed her once again.

Morag assured Davina ate something anytime she stirred. The maid was a slip of a thing. Davina was not tall, but she thought Morag would only come to her chin. Her size made it hard to judge her age, making her appear more a child than a grown woman. She wore her light hair that was kissed with a bit of red in a single plait down her back. Was it an indication she was married, or just the easiest way to attend her work? Morag's hair reminded her of Rachel. The young woman Nathair had tried to assault. Davina had told Rachel as she's sent the maid away it was for her own good, but Davina herself would die if she had to face the same fate. In all that Davina considered, death still seemed like the best option.

Davina didn't ask after Morag. She didn't want to know anyone when she had no intention of staying. She ate the thin stew and nibbled on a bit of cheese, if for no other reason than to gain enough strength to flee. Sleeping through most of her first day in the Kincaid manse helped more than the food.

The following day, she ate a little more as she willed her strength to return.

"How are ye feeling this fine day, m'lady?" Morag pushed open one set of shutters.

The air was heavy, dry, and devoid of life. Though it had a bite, no breeze touched her. The only sound was of the squawk of crows, instead of the call of gulls, kittiwakes, and corncrakes. She couldn't stay here.

"M'lady?"

"Fine," she mumbled.

Morag looked at her, head cocked, her lips pursed in confusion. "Well, ye are lookin' stronger." She straightened Davina's covers and sat the tray beside her on the bed. "I'm sure ye're eager to get out of this bed and meet yer betrothed. Every lass is jealous."

They can have him and he them. Davina tried to rise to drink the watered wine, but air hissed through her clenched teeth and pain arrested her movements.

"Let me help." Morag reached for the cup and held Davina's head to assist her in drinking.

After only a few bits, Davina turned her head and pretended to sleep again. Morag left the chamber. She didn't return for several hours. The sun was already setting when the maid appeared in the room again.

"The Yule starts in a few days. Ye'll want to be hale enough to join the party in the hall. Oh, to be wed in this joyous season. Is it not grand?" Morag chattered without noticing if Davina even attended to her words.

A deep chill returned with the rising moon and the shutters were at last closed. Leaving at night was impossible. But could she slip away unseen during the day? She'd have to find a way.

The following day, Davina noted the coming and going of Morag and the other maids. Davina didn't even try to learn their names. After each meal, they left her for at least a couple of hours to rest. She'd try to slip away after midday on the morrow.

Chapter 32

Davina ate a larger portion of stew the next day.

"Ye'll be dinin' with yer husband for the Yule and Christ Mass festivities," Morag chirped as Davina reclined back and closed her eyes.

She listened as the maid removed the chamber pot and returned with it emptied a few moments later. Morag gathered up her dishes next and eased out of the room with a soft click of the latch.

When the room grew still and quiet, Davina worked herself to sit on the side of the bed. Breathing hard from the effort, Davina remained there for a while. She tried to remove her nightclothes, but bringing her arms up to pull the garment over her head was torture. The painful pulling of the stitches in her side also kept her from standing straight.

With slow shuffled steps, she made it to one window and pushed open the wood coverings. Rolling, tree-covered hills greeted her. A solid wall around the manse lay closer, below her window. She moved to the other window. More trees, though those closest to the keep lay in neat rows. The apple trees filled an area just outside the wall. And a door sat open in the surrounding wall, just below her window.

Davina found a wool cloak in the wardrobe, wrapped it around her, and raised the cowl without crying out. With her feet in house slippers almost a size too big, she worked her way to the door of her small chamber. A quick glance revealed it had no bathing chamber. But then, here, she was not the lady of the manse. Just an unwanted bride.

She eased the door open and released a breath when she found no guard at the door. Using the wall for support, she inched along the corridor, listening for anyone. She made it down only two stairs. Her legs quaked enough that she feared she'd careen to her death. She sat and slid down to rest on her rump. Maybe it would be for the best if it all came to a quick end.

Voices grew as she spotted another hallway at the bottom. She hugged close to the wall as two men passed. Their conversation faded and light flooded where they'd been. A door to the outside lay not far away. Encouraged she'd made it this far, and knowing that the way out was on the same side as the orchard gate, strengthened her enough to scoot down each step until she reached the bottom and stood.

Her feet dragged down the passageway to her escape hatch. The sun was on its way to the western horizon but it still made her squint against its brightness. She only had another hour of decent light before the short winter day would encase her in night.

Davina blinked and glanced around again, still she found no one standing about. Could God at last be showing her a bit of kindness? Without a wall or anything to hold to, her steps were slow and unsteady. She staggered through the gate and leaned against the wall. Her head lulled back with a thud against the stone. At this pace, how far could she get before it became too dark to proceed? What if the cold claimed her? Did she taste snow in the air? It seldom snowed at Seycoll as it lay on the sea, but this small manse sat far inland and higher in the mountains. She pulled the thin borrowed cloak tight about her, hiding her fingers in the folds.

Forward. She needed to get moving and keep pushing forward as long as she could. Davina knew if she stopped, she'd most likely die. Something told her that not even the Lord Himself would welcome her into the heavenlies.

The man was insufferable. Da incessant ordering about had cause a riff between father and son. Callen wasn't the eldest, but he was a grown man. He wouldn't inherit anything of Father's. He had to make his own way in the world. Yet Da kept forcing him to bend a knee.

Marry! Had the man gone daft? More likely, Callen would have to join the priesthood if he wanted any actual power or influence. Da had refused to send him to the monastery when he was younger. Now, they waited for his brother Dougal's return from fighting alongside the king. There'd be no place in his own home for Callen with Dougal inside Bottleigh, too.

Callen growled his frustration as he stomped through the orchard.

A bride! By the sword, he was not ready to be coddling a faint lass and providing for hungry bairns. Aye, he was two score and five, but he didn't even know where he'd get a meal once he left the manse. He was skilled with horses and many came to him to break their young mounts, but having enough to provide for a family would be unthinkable.

Movement caught his eye. Few people came to the orchard after the harvest. With the snows threatening, the servants had plucked all the apples weeks ago.

The dark shrouded form staggered from tree to tree, barely making it to the next without falling. Who of his kirth and kin would be so ale-washed this early in the evening?

A sheer white fabric peeked out below the cloak. A woman? Dressed in her sleeping gown? Was she also missing a shoe?

Callen inched closer. The figure slumped against a broad trunk and sunk to the ground. Her head tipped back and a wisp of flaming red hair danced in the breeze. No lass he knew in Bottleigh had hair that color.

But *she* did. The one chosen to be his bride. Wasn't she too injured to get out of bed? This woman was up to something. He'd figure it out and use it to convince Da she was not the woman for him.

"Where're ye headed, lass?"

Each panted breath huffed out in a cloud in the cold air. "Away."

Callen approached her from behind and to her right. He couldn't yet see her face. "What makes ye flee?"

Her words came in pants. "The kind Laird Malcolm thought—I would be—a good match for—his son. But the younger—laird doesn't wish—to wed me."

She'd heard. Somehow, she knew how he felt about their marriage. "So ye run away to punish the cruel man?"

"Nay!" A vehement shake of her head caused more of the cowl to fall away from her face. "Oh, please don't think ill—of yer laird. He is a good—and honorable man. His people—love him—and speak well of him always. 'Tis not his fault. 'Tis me. He wants better than me as a bride —and I can't fault him. I wish him—nothing but the best. When I'm gone—he can choose a lass—he favors."

Callen now struggled to breathe. His heart clenched. She spoke well of him. Wanted his best. He'd refused to even meet her and railed at the idea of a union with her. Yet here she fled into the growing night, ill dressed, and still weak from the attack that had left her with a knife in her side, only desiring his happiness.

He knelt beside her. "Lass, how good or honorable can I be for refusing ye without at least meeting ye?"

"Oh." She gasped and stretched out her hand toward him as her face turned. Blood coated her fingertips.

His gaze flickered from her bloody hand as he caught sight of her pale skin sprinkled with a thousand freckles and became caught by her ice-blue eyes. By the sword, she was a vision.

"Go m'laird. No one'll know ye saw me."

"I'll know, lass. Come, let's get ye back to yer bed."

She pressed the back of her hand against his chest to prevent staining his clothes with her bloody fingers. "I'll not hold ye to yer father's agreement with Fergus. Go in peace and may God bless ye with all good things." Her head sagged back against the tree again and her eyes slid closed.

He wanted to be forever bound to the contract to wed this woman as he had wanted nothing before in his life. He tried to lower her hand and pick her up.

Her head tossed one last time. "Go, ye're free of me."

Callen waited just a moment more as her hand dropped and snatched her up into his arms. "Lord, may it never be that I am free again. Help her." He raced within the walls and toward the back stairs. "Get Iain and Morag," he ordered the first person to cross his path. "Send them to the lady's chamber at once."

Chapter 33

The Kincaid healer had raced to tend Davina, but it took far too long to stanch the bleeding. Within hours, her fever spiked.

Iain raked his arm across his forehead to sop up the sweat. His gaze was grave as he looked at Callen. "I've done what I can, m'laird. I fear she is too weak to survive all she's been through." Iain's wispy gray hair fluttered with his shaking head.

"I'll not lose hope." Callen sat on a stool beside Davina's bed and caressed her heart-shaped face with a damp cloth. "And ye won't quit tryin' to aid her."

"Of course not," the physician said.

Morag changed the water in the basin Callen used when it grew warm and made sure the men had something to eat and drink as they stayed with her through the night. Her moans and whimpers as her head tossed about stirred a fear in Callen worse than any battle he'd charged into.

Her muddled words were unintelligible, but Callen couldn't deny she suffered in deep pain. And her fever raged until she had soaked through all her bedding.

Come daybreak, she stilled and quieted. "She improves," Callen said with renewed hope.

"Nay, m'laird. She is near gone. The fever is too great."

"Morag!" The maid jerked awake from where she dozed in the corner at Callen's shout. "We need a large tub and water from the loch— snow too, if it is close enough—in all due haste."

The woman fled the room at a full run.

Iain put his fingers to Davina's throat, lifted an eyelid, and touched her forehead. "I doubt she'll live long enough for ye to try such a rash treatment."

"I'll not have ye talk so. If ye can't hold yer tongue, ye can leave. But I'll not stop fightin' for her." He threw off her sheet and poured all the water they had over her.

"Callen?"

His father stood in the doorway.

"Iain, help her," Callen said as he moved to speak to his da in the hallway.

"What happened?" Da's gaze searched his.

"She heard of what I said to ye, Da. That I didn't want to marry her. She tried to leave, but the action reopened her wound and, now, infection has set in. Iain fears the worst."

Da's face crinkled. "Have ye been with her all night?"

Callen turned and glanced over his shoulder at Davina. Her thin, wet night rail clung to her flesh and her flaming hair spread over the pillow. "I can't leave her. She thinks she's not wanted."

"Ye've changed yer mind, then?" Da's words were not angry or smug, but curious.

Callen paced a few steps away and rotated his head back and forth until the muscles in his neck loosened. He hated admitting he'd been wrong—even worse was acknowledging that his da was right. "She welcomed death, that I might be happy. With what may end up being her last words, she called blessings down upon me. She's not some preening grand lady who wishes her every childish desire fulfilled. To her detriment, she wants nothing but me best. How can I not desire such a wife?"

Da didn't remark on his victory. "Yer mother and I will pray. What else do ye require?"

"I've sent Morag to get a chilled bath ready."

"I'll make sure we do all in the utmost haste."

The men nodded to one another. They would say no more about this moment.

The dull ache of pain dragged Davina from oblivion. She'd been right; God hadn't wanted her either. She drifted through the soreness. Her limbs were heavy. Hair stuck to her face. There didn't seem to be anywhere she didn't hurt. If she could shift positions, move her muscles to work them loose, perhaps the pain would subside. Her left arm slid across the bedding with ease, but her right wouldn't budge. Something warm tightened around it. Davina struggled to twist her body to roll to her side. Bolts of searing pain tore through her. She bit her lip to stifle the scream.

She lay still. What happened? Nathair. He'd attacked her—no, his father. She'd gotten in the way. But that was days ago, wasn't it? The itchy hair glued to her face annoyed her. Again, she pulled her right hand to brush it away. The warmth of another hand tightened on it.

Davina pried her eyes open. Where was she? A boat ride at night. They had forced her to leave Seycoll. Where had Fergus sent her? Laird Malcolm.

Something moved to her right. A head, covered in brown curls to the collar, rose from where it had rested on the side of her bed. The light from the candles around the room revealed auburn mixed in with the darker shade. A man, with a full beard of the same russet color as his hair, yawned and rolled his broad shoulders as he straightened in his chair. His hazel gaze settled on her. And he smiled. He brought her hand he held to his lips and pressed a kiss to her knuckles.

Did she know him?

He brushed her hair from her face with a calloused hand. "Lass, ye near scared the life out of me." The wrinkles on his cheek from where it had rested on her bedcoverings caused odd shadows on his face. "How are ye feelin'?"

No moisture lay in her mouth. She tried to swallow, but the dust didn't move. Her tongue remained lifeless, stuck in a parched desert.

"Here." He released her hand, brought a cup to her lips, and cradled her head. "Better?"

She gave a single nod. "Who?" The lone word came out a hoarse whisper, made her cough, and sent bolts of pain through her so she didn't have the strength to try again.

"Ye, don't remember me?" His shoulders sagged, but he helped her drink again. "We met in the orchard a couple evenings ago."

Orchard? Apples. She had staggered through the apple trees to … Where had she been going?

As if reading her confusion, he said, "Ye were runnin' away."

Yes, she knew she'd needed to leave. Why? Marriage. Fergus and Malcolm had arranged for her to wed Malcolm's son. She looked at the man next to her bed again. The son. The man who'd said he didn't want the marriage or her? Why was he here now?

A petite woman with blonde hair that looked like she had dipped it in strawberry juice slipped into the room. Davina knew her. What was her name? Why were her thoughts so muddled?

"Morag, fetch Iain," the man said.

"Aye, m'laird." She left Davina alone with the man. Against her wishes, he'd collected her hand once more. Without the strength to even lift her head, she couldn't stop him. As much as she had always wanted contact with another, she needed to get this man to let her go.

She let her eyes close, wishing for the nothingness of sleep again. Things were simpler there.

Another kiss pressed to the back of her hand. "Promise ye'll stay with me," he whispered.

She looked at him. Was this Malcolm's son who'd sworn to never wed her or even meet her? Had another in Malcolm's home chosen to claim Davina? Oh, by the saints, she was sore and tired. She again fought to move.

"What do ye require, lass?"

"To move?"

"Where do ye aim to go this time?"

She shook her head. "I just need to move. I'm stiff."

His hands slid down her body and rolled her so she faced him. He caressed her face and kissed her temple. "Better?"

Not really. Her skin was on fire, cheeks ablaze. She couldn't breathe. And none of it had anything to do with her injury. This man was taking great liberties. "Why?"

"Why, what?"

"Are ye here?"

"Is a husband not to tend to his wife when a grave illness befalls his love? In sickness and health, as they say."

"M'laird? A thin-haired man stepped into the room. "By the sword, she's still alive."

Davina glanced at the gray-haired man in a rumpled tunic. He held her face and looked deep into her eyes. Lying on her side as she was, it put a crick in her neck. She tried to pull free of him, but when that failed, she attempted to push him away.

The man claiming to be her husband, though she didn't remember saying any rites, put his hand on Iain's arm. "Ye're frightening her. She doesn't remember us."

Iain nodded. "It has been known to happen. Such a prolonged fever can affect the memory." He moved to examine her side and Davina fought to grab her bedclothes close again.

Her 'husband' took both her hands in his and held them steady. "Iain's our doctor. He needs to check yer injury. Do ye remember?"

"Nathair." Heat filled her face as hands touched the bare skin of her side. How undressed was she with only these men in her chamber? She dared a glance at what the healer did. A hole was cut in her night rail, about the size of a man's hand. Otherwise, her gown provided a modest covering.

Iain removed the cloth protecting her wound. "It looks to be healing. I'll add more ointment and redress it."

"Might our lady bathe before ye do?" Morag had appeared at the end of the bed as if from vapor. "It would do her good to be clean and to change the bedding as well."

Iain agreed.

Morag looked at Davina's 'husband.' Oh, how she wished she at least knew this man's name. "All is prepared."

Her husband nodded and drew back all her covers. She braced her hands against his chest as his arms slid under her. But her strength was no match for his. He kissed her forehead. "Don't fret. I'll not be staying. The maids will have to see to yer needs—at least until we speak the consents."

So, they weren't married, not in the eyes of God. Did that make him carrying her dressed in a sheer gown to a bath worse? Yet she couldn't deny how, on the one hand, his tender hold touched her heart; but on the other it distressed her to the point she was gasping for each breath. A tiny part of her wanted to throw her arms around his neck and bury her face in his collar, while the rest of her wanted to leap out of his arms. Thankfully, she hadn't the strength for either rash behavior.

He carried her to the chamber across the hall. A gaggle of women and a steaming tub awaited her. He sat her on a bench beside it, kissed the top of her head, and turned to the door. "Take excellent care of her and call when she's ready."

"Aye, m'laird."

She trembled when he was gone. Did she miss him? Perhaps it was the loss of heat from his well-carved body she lacked.

Chapter 34

With care, and far too many hands, the maids worked her out of her night rail and into the water.

"Oh, how ye gave Laird Callen such a fright, m'lady."

"I've never seen him in such a dither."

"Nay, never."

So, it was Callen, Malcolm's son. What had changed his mind? Why did he insist they marry now? "Why?" The maids almost missed her question amongst their chatter.

"'Tis an odd question, m'lady. The laird is beyond smitten, of course."

"What happened?" It made little sense that he refused her before they met, and then he attested to being smitten. Emotions—especially in men—didn't change that radically.

"He found ye bleeding and chilled in the orchard," Morag said.

Another older brunette picked up the tale. "No one knows why ye were out wandering about when ye were so injured."

A young blonde spoke next. "Some suspect ye were driven mad by the fever."

"But Laird Callen found ye in time. Saints be praised," Morag concluded.

"Rushed ye back, hollering for the doctor. Never left yer side after that." The brunette smiled.

The maids worked to clean her body and hair as Davina fought to attend to the conversations that each took a part in telling. Saints, she was tired.

They drew her from the water, dried her with soft towels, redressed her wound, and pulled a clean night rail over her head. They sat her by the fire and Morag dried her hair as the rest tidied the room and left to prepare her bed.

Davina couldn't keep her head up as sleep fought to claim her.

"I'll fetch the laird," Morag said.

"We needn't bother him," Davina protested.

"Do ye find me unworthy, m'lady?"

Davina stared at her.

"Laird Callen has given me strict orders to fetch him when ye're ready to return to yer chamber. He'll have me hide if I fail to follow his orders." The woman looked stricken, eyes wide, hand at her throat.

"Is he so cruel?"

"Nay, but where ye are concerned, all must be done as he requests."

Davina waved her hand for the maid to proceed. Exhaustion prevented her from continuing to argue. She didn't recall Morag leaving her side, but Davina lay cradled in Callen's arms again. "Ye smell like harebell. Me favorite of all the highland flowers." He kissed her temple.

When she woke, a single candle flickered. Callen still sat by her bed, head resting on the covers, where he held her hand tight within his. He stirred as she tried again to roll to her side. He helped her get comfortable and then caressed her hand with his thumb until sleep claimed her.

"I thank God He spared ye, love."

Over the next few days, Callen was there any time she opened her eyes. He either sat beside her bed or stood near the windows. But he was never far and was quick to come to her. He helped her drink and even fed her. Morag remained near, but it was Callen who attended her.

But every time she looked at him, she remembered his bellowed words from the night she arrived: "I don't want her."

One morn, she woke to no one in her chamber. She staggered out of bed and into the hall. Voices below drove her up the stairs, where she stumbled to a door that led out onto the battlements. A harsh wind lashed at her robe and tugged her hair. A few men stood near a stairway that led down into the courtyard. She turned and looked out over the wall. It was high enough that a fall would kill her.

She tried to pull herself up.

"Am I such a monster that ye'd wish yer own death, lass?"

She startled and fell back. Callen was there to catch her before she slammed into the wall behind her. Looking up into his eyes, she saw nothing but pain. "Ye said ye didn't—"

His fingers covered her mouth. "I was being a petulant child. It had nothin' to do with ye, Davina."

Why did her name on his lips send tingles dancing down her spine?

"Had I been the one to travel to Seycoll and meet ye first, I'd have insisted Fergus allow us to wed that very day. I'd not have cared what me da said. But because Da was the one to arrange it without me knowledge, I rejected the offer out of hand. Da and I have a tumultuous relationship. I sore regret it has caused ye pain, lass."

She searched his face. His earnest words pleaded with her.

"Do ye know what day it is?"

She shook her head.

"The Christ Mass. I joined the service to thank the Lord for ye and Morag went to fetch ye some sweets. Would ye mark this most holy day by doing somethin' so dreadful and heartbreakin' or will ye say the consents with me?"

"Words mean nothing. I've said them twice before and it's all come to naught."

His thumb brushed over her cheek. "And glad I am for that." He kissed her temple. "Will ye come to the kirk?"

She closed her eyes. Could she go through this again? This time with a man who'd refused her to get back at his father? "Are ye sure I am the one ye want?"

His smile, the steady hold of his gaze, the fierceness with which he held her hands gave further conviction to the weight of his words. "I've never been surer of anythin' in me life."

"Why?" She shook her head. He made no sense. He knew nothing of her.

"Ye showed yer love for me before we met. Even now, ye seek what ye think is for me best, though it would destroy me to lose ye. How can I not meet a love like that in kind?"

She shivered in the thin robe she'd thrown over her shoulders before leaving her chamber.

His hands tightened on hers as his stare bore into her. "Will ye marry me, Davina?"

Could she trust him? Did any part of her shattered heart remain to give to this man? Could she dare to hope again? Were any other choices open to her?

"Please?"

His smile grew as she gave a single nod.

Callen carried her to her chamber with a *whoop*. Morag helped her into a simple gown. And Callen returned to carry her down the stairs all the way to the kirk. They didn't stop on the steps outside, but entered and knelt before the altar.

"I need ye to make a vow before the others arrive, Davina." His voice was heavy and grave.

Her heart beat even harder until it pounded in her ears so she struggled to hear his next words.

"Swear before our Lord, ye will never again, with purpose or through neglect, try to harm yerself or take yer life."

Davina looked up at the altar and the gold crucifix of the Lord atop it.

"Swear this, my love. I can't be with ye every moment, nor can I continue to worry over ye. Please, do this for me."

She swallowed hard and struggled to form the words. Said here, before the altar, she could never break this vow. Come what may in the next moments, she'd have to live with the consents she was about to make, reguardless of Callen true desire. "I swear never, by purpose or neglect, to seek me own harm or death."

Subdued but joyful voices filled the kirk like the incoming tide. A priest in ornate robes stood in front of the kneeling couple. Now, the third time she'd said these words, this time felt different. All Seycoll had believed she married Fergus to provide them a better heir. And she'd said her first vows in such haste, she scarcely tasted them before they were spent. But this time seemed more real—holy, almost.

Callen took her hands as he turned on his knees. His adoring gaze washed over her like a spring rain, quickening her pulse again. "I take ye, Davina of the Moffat, to be me wife. In sickness or hale, 'till death does part us." He spoke his consent so bold, and commanding, it sent a shiver through her entire body

She answered and hoped the uncertainty wasn't noticeable in her promise. "I take ye, Callen of the Kincaid, as me husband. In sickness and hale, 'till death does part us."

"As you each gave these vows without reservation or compulsion, before those assembled as witnesses in this holy house, God will honor them; and let no man tear asunder what He has brought together." The priest closed with a prayer and a blessing.

Those gathered filed out as Callen helped her to her feet. She swayed for a moment as his sure arm held her steady. "There is but one more thing."

She looked up at Callen. What more was there to a wedding than speaking the rites? He led her outside, where two of his clan held a broom a few inches off the ground.

Callen whispered in her ear. "Will ye sweep away the past and start a new life with me, Davina? Will ye jump the besom?"

He took her hand, and they walked toward the broom. His right hand held hers as his left arm encircled her waist and helped her clear the obstacle without danger and little pain.

With all his kirth and kin cheering around them, he cradled her face and pressed his lips to hers. They were warm and soft and his moustache tickled and poked. His tongue skimmed the slit between her lips as the people cheered. He nipped at her lower lip and withdrew at last.

She gasped for breath. Her head spun, and she realized she held his tunic in a fearsome grip. Heat flamed against her face as the cheering grew into ruckus chants for him to kiss her again. She ducked her head, not allowing him access, mortified by the brazen show of affection in front of so many.

But he raised her chin with a finger and kissed her again; this time tender and gentle, but with no less passion. Her body hummed with a wild energy she didn't understand.

Chapter 35

Davina struggled to catch her breath after Callen's heated kisses. He again carried her, but they didn't return to the keep. Instead, he climbed the dais and set her at the high table before taking his place to her left. Laird Malcolm and his wife were on his other side.

"What a glorious day," Laird Malcolm said as everyone sat and the trestle tables in the space below filled. Dirks, and feasting knives thumped against the boards. Davina stifled a shudder. "Not only have we celebrated the Yule this morn, the coming of our Lord as a wee bairn, but Laird Callen and Lady Davina have joined their lives as husband and wife. I couldn't be prouder. Me kin, let us feast well this day!"

The cheers rattled the dinnerware.

Davina had wed—again. Was she now a wife twice, or thrice? What would it mean to be married to this man now placing tasty items on her plate? The tenderest slices of meat, a few bits of the cheese she favored, and several holiday sweets. He gave her the best.

But hadn't Fergus done the same from the very beginning? He'd piled her plate high with an obscene amount of food—*before* they said the rites. No, Fergus had wanted to talk in the solar. The clan had formed a path to the kirk. He only said that he took her. But he never said 'wife.' She'd not taken notice of this omission. What would Fergus have told her if they had spoken before they uttered those words? Before the revelry and dancing that lasted long into the night?

"Davina?" A hand tightened over her arm, pulling her from her memories. "Are ye ta right?"

The emotion playing on Callen's face startled her. His gaze caressed her, his forehead crinkled, his lips almost hid within his beard.

She nodded.

"They celebrate ye," he pointed out at the jovial folks, "as they do the Yule and the Christ-child. But I only celebrate ye."

She glanced at the Kincaid clan. "I shouldn't replace Christ, m'laird," she mumbled.

He leaned until he brushed their shoulders; his breath brushed her ear. "We are wed lass, ye must call me by me name."

She winced as she reached for her feasting knife; her side ached and her memory of the last she'd seen a meal knife doubled the pain. Her fingers trembled over the handle.

Callen took it, sliced her meat in bites small enough for a wee child, and moved the would-be weapon to the far side of his plate. He kissed her hand and reached for his fork.

Had Fergus kissed her? Until Nathair attacked he hadn't touched her, other than when her hand sat atop his as they went to the service on the Lord's Day.

"Are ye too tired to eat? I can return ye to yer chamber."

She shook her head. Or did she nod? "My thoughts are on a bit of an adventure, I fear. I can't seem to pen them in."

Callen chuckled. It was bright and cheerful. Then he pressed a quick kiss to her cheek. "Oh, I am glad ye consented, lass."

She considered him. His smile couldn't be contained.

"I can only pray ye take half as much pleasure in looking on me as I do gazing at ye, love." He kissed her lips, leaving the flavors of roasted boar and berry tarts behind. "Ye need to eat."

This man confused her, sent her emotions on a violent wind, and made her entire body behave in an foreign manner.

After the meal, minstrels and jugglers performed. The people dismantled the trestle tables to make room for dancing. The second time Davina yawned, Callen gave his apologies to his parents and carried her up to her chamber. He left her with Morag and didn't return until the following morn to fetch her for the breaking of the fast.

As before, a sennight passed as a bride, but she had yet to be a wife. It took her near as long to convince Callen she was well enough to descend the stairs without being carried.

"Ye'll wait for me, love. I don't want ye falling." He entwined their arms and struggled to walk beside her on the narrow, twisting stairs.

There was little difference between being Fergus' ward and Callen's wife. Save that in Bottleigh, she was not the lady of the manse. Callen's mother held that honor, leaving Davina with nothing to do with her time locked up in the dreary keep. Without glass windows, the shutters remained closed and covered with heavy tapestries against the frosty wind and frequent snow flurries.

When she'd slept most of her days, it had not been such a burden. But as she healed, she paced like a caged animal awaiting slaughter. How was she to endure years' worth of winters in this place?

One morning dawned under bright rays of the sun and melted the thin skiff of snow from the night before. The wind was light, but she slid into her long leather cloak all the same. Stepping out on the battlements once more, she wandered along their firm stones and looked out over the tree-covered land. And other than a small frozen loch lying almost hidden to the north, that was all she saw—trees and more trees.

Why was she here? It didn't seem Callen wanted her as a wife any more than Fergus or Ealar. She had no purpose.

"Davina?"

She turned her back more fully toward Callen and swiped at a tear.

"Ye aren't goin' back on yer vow?" There was an edge to his question.

She shook her head.

"What troubles ye, love?" He was closer, just over her shoulder. His heavy plea warmed her cheek.

"I'm well." Her words didn't even convince her.

He grasped her shoulder, turned her to face him, and raised her head with his finger. "Yer tears would say otherwise." He brushed away another with his thumb.

She searched his face. "Do ye regret saying the consents before yer kirth and kin?"

Callen straightened, taking a step back as if she'd struck him. "By the sword, why would ye ask such a thing?"

She tried to turn, but he wouldn't allow her to move. "I'm no more a wife to ye than I was to Fergus' or Ealar."

His shoulders relaxed, his eyes darkened, and he removed one glove to caress her cheek. He pulled her to him, lowered his head, and claimed her lips. Like the first time, the powerful kiss sought her with a hunger she didn't understand. His tongue prodded until she opened her mouth to him. His scent of the crisp air and horses filled her, and he tasted like roast meat.

One hand worked to unfasten her cloak, and his hands slid inside. With splayed fingers he explored her ribs, slipping down her sides, yet never released her lips. His hand covered her wound, and he gave her side a gentle squeeze.

She drew from him with a gasp. Panting and heart pounding, she stared at him.

Callen closed her cloak, took her hands in his warm gloved ones, and leaned his forehead against hers. His eyes closed, and he seemed to fight to slow his own breathing. "I ache for ye, lass, like nothing I've ever known. But I don't avoid yer bed for any other reason than the pain ye still endure. This is the only thing preventing me from coming to ye, Ina."

She pulled back, and her head tipped to the side as she looked at him. The feelings he stirred inside her. To be held, kissed, touched like he'd done, made her dizzy. But it had ended before she could savor it. She wanted to be back in his arm. At the moment, she didn't care about the pain. If he'd just hold her like that again.

"Do ye not favor me calling ye that?"

Calling her what? She blinked and tried to recall the words he'd spoken while she floated on the sensation his touch had left. Ina. That's what he'd called her. "Me mum called me Ina as a wee lass. She was the only one. It was her way of telling me she loved me."

His grip tightened as she shivered. "I can't imagine anyone loving ye as much as I. And I am desperate to be with ye." He claimed her lips again with a quick kiss but he didn't hold her. "But Ina, I'll not cause ye pain. Ye've seen far more than is right. And I love ye too much to put me needs afore yers." He held out his arm and waited.

Her body still hummed from what he'd done. Everything about this man differed from the others. She wanted to trust him, to believe in his claims of love. But more she wanted to be held like he'd done and never let go. She pushed that long unmet desire away, and with a quaking step, she moved forward and linked her arm with his. He drew her close and kissed her temple.

"Ye will heal soon enough and ye won't have reason to doubt."

Her body relaxed as he led her back into the warmth of the keep.

Chapter 36

Callen still didn't have Davina's trust. He had yet to convince her of his genuine desire to have her as his wife. He noticed her hesitance to take his hand, the surprise when he kissed her, and noted the way her gaze searched his for any hint of doubt he may have.

Callen stomped up the stairs from her chamber. He wanted to punch the wall and erase his cruel words from her memory. Of all the remembrances of coming to Bottleigh, she had lost to the fever, why did that one insist on plaguing her?

Callen approached the family solar. Da had asked him to come, but he'd spotted Davina on the wall and rushed to her. There was a mare about to foal. He needed to check on her, but Da had requested his presence, so here he came, like an obedient lapdog.

"Are ye sure about her? She seems troubled," Mum asked Da as Callen approached the room.

"She is not the lass I met at Seycoll. I thought once she recovered from Nathair's attack." Da paused. "It's like the villain drained the life from her."

Callen pushed open one door and slipped inside.

"Ah, Callen, good. Ye've arrived." Da inclined his head.

"Da." He nodded to his mother and poured himself a little scotch before sitting.

"I've been wanting to talk to ye, but with concerns for Davina, there hasn't been the time. While I was at the market, members of both the Macay and Gunn spoke to me about breeding their mares with yer studs. Along with payment, they promise to each return a filly."

Callen had thought to reach out to their near neighbors on the same matter. "The clans have solid stock. They would produce well."

"I imagine yer keen on starting yer own stable now. Would be a wise move," Da confirmed, which only made Callen want to do the exact opposite.

Of course, it would be a sound business opportunity. Callen knew horseflesh like no one else in this part of the highlands. His garron ponies were known for their size, strength, and temperament; which is why these clans sought to breed their stalk with them. Did Da think him daft? He swallowed his ire and gave a silent nod.

"How is Davina settling in?" His mum sought to ease the tension between father and son, as usual.

"She's healing, but not as quick as she would prefer." He wouldn't say more. By the conversation when he entered, they already feared she wasn't fit.

"Then she is like the rest of us." Da laughed. "She'll be fine once the weather breaks and she can stretch her legs a bit."

"A little fresh air might do her some good now," Mum added.

Callen would keep his own council on his wife. "As soon as there is a decent break in the snow, I'll take a couple of stallions up to the Gunn first."

Da nodded his approval as Callen drained his cup. "If there is nothing else?"

"Thank ye, lad. I'll leave ye to yer tasks."

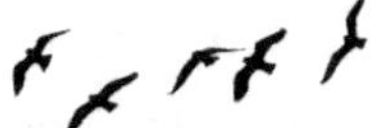

Callen hadn't joined them at the morning meal; something about a horse giving birth. Davina didn't understand why, as the laird's son, Callen needed to be present. She shrugged and sat in his chair as his mum indicated. Laird Malcolm filled her plate after his wife's and they ate with neither talking to her. Far fewer were present at the early morning meal than had been at the celebration the previous evenings. The Yule celebrations were, at last, winding down. With the Christ Mass and the wedding added in, the good folk of Bottleigh had found an excuse to continue the revelry for another sennight.

As the meal concluded, Lady Kincaid rose. "Davina, would ye join me?"

"Of course, m'lady." Davina stood and followed.

Callen's mum took Davina's hand and smiled. "We are family now, ye must call me Freya."

"Thank ye."

"Are ye well enough to manage the climb?"

"Aye." Davina was slow, but her strength was returning. Freya was a hand shorter than Callen, with deep brown hair. There were strands of auburn, like Callen's, and a few of gray. She wore it plaited and wound into a bun. She had a womanly figure and, while she was not fat, neither was she slender.

Davina followed Freya past her room and up to the third floor. They stepped through double doors into a small seating area.

"The family solar. I hope we can spend many evenings here together. Callen has been reluctant. It is far too common for he and his da to end the night arguing. But I'm praying between the two of us we can assure they tame their bull-headed ways."

Davina stared at her. "I doubt I'll be of much help. I hold little sway over Callen."

Freya jerk so the pitcher she pour the drink from almost missed the cup. "Oh, lass. Ye don't understand the effect ye've had on me son. I've never seen him so focused, driven, and selfless. Ye've made him a better man already." She handed a cup to Davina and pointed to a wooden frame strung with yarn on a table before the fire.

"Malcolm tells me ye learned weaving before coming to Fergus?"

"Aye, m'l—Yes," Davina stuttered to correct herself.

"Have ye ever worked on one of these?"

"A table loom? Nay. I've seen one, but I spent most of my time on the larger wall looms."

"Oh, those big monstrosities take a dreadful-long time to complete. We use this to create our plaids." Freya fingered the one draped over her shoulders like a shawl. "I thought I could teach ye the pattern and we could share some of the long winter hours."

Davina nodded, grateful to have something to occupy her time, but wary of the real reason Callen's mother wished to speak with her.

They sat side-by-side, comparing technique and sipping on their drinks. The wine was a bit tart. Davina missed the mead Fergus always offered her.

"Do ye love me son?"

There it was. The true purpose of this meeting. Davina drained her cup, coughing at the sourness, and stood. She moved toward a tapestry, drew it aside, and cracked open a shutter. The bitter wind cooled her face and calmed her queasy stomach.

She watched the few snowflakes drift toward the ground and vanish. "I want to." It was true. She wanted to love someone and be loved in return. "But I'm afraid."

Freya didn't comment. She'd stopped her weaving to watch and listen.

Davina turned back to the storm trying to make its presence known. How she felt like those futile snowflakes. "I tried very hard to love me da. But he wanted a son to join him in his trade, lighten his burden, and carry on his name. I was never enough for him. He sold me off to Ealar, and though he was fat and old, I determined I would love him as a good wife ought. But he died rather than claim me. Da said it was me fault." Davina shrugged and rubbed at her arm. "Then he took me to Fergus. And I loved him and all his people with my whole heart. He told me from me first night that I be only a wife in name, but he was kind, generous, and gentle. Something Da never was." She swiped at a tear before the chilled air could harden it. "When Fergus sent me away …" She had to stop, for she couldn't control her tears. After a few moments, she closed the shutters and turned to look at Freya. "Me heart shattered in a thousand shards. I don't know if I can love again. And if I could, what would become of me when Callen sent me away also?"

Freya offered her a gentle smile. "And what if ye found the love ye sought?"

Davina leaned against the wall and stared at the tapestry covering the window. "Could I ever trust it?"

Freya stood, draped her arm over Davina's shoulder, and led her back to the fire. "Time will tell. For now, we'd best warm ye. If I let ye catch a chill, Callen would never forgive me." She offered a mischievous smirk, and it pulled at Davina until she wanted to lift her lips as well.

Chapter 37

"How's the newest member of the Kincaid herd?"

Callen looked up at his mother. She never came to the stables. Even now, her nose wrinkled.

Callen rested on his forearms on the top rail of the pin where the new pony nursed. "A bonny strong filly. She'll make fine breeding stock in a few years."

"Might ye have a minute to talk?" Mum paused and bent to stroke the wee horse through the rails.

"Aye." Callen ladled some water onto his hands and wiped them clean before donning his gloves and following Mum out into the courtyard. The morning snow flurries had given way to clear skies under a weak sun.

"I spent the morning with Davina." Mum watched the path ahead of them.

Callen almost stopped dead. Heaven help them if Mum suggested he send her away.

Mum smiled and looped her arm in his. "I like her very much. Yer Da made a wise choice. She is forthright, honest, and intelligent. And she is good for ye."

"Why do I feel as though there is a 'however,' coming?"

"Do ye remember the summer ye found the eaglet?"

Callen held up his gloved hand. "Remember it? I still have the scars from that ungrateful wee cur."

Mum pressed on. "Do ye recall why it behaved so cruelly when ye but wanted to help it survive?"

Callen let his memory drift to those long days past. "He was frightened. I was rather large compared to him. And he thought I meant him harm." What did a saved eaglet have to do with his wife?

She glanced at him with a smirk that told him she had a point he was being dull to grasp. "And how did ye earn his trust?"

Callen chuckled. "Hours clear on to a fortnight of coaxin' him to eat and talkin' to him."

"Yer kindness at last won him over," Mum concluded with a smile and a raised chin.

Callen stopped and stared at his mum.

She squeezed his hand. "Ye've rescued another wee bird, me son."

"What?"

"This time ye've gotten a gentle dove. But she's just as frightened. It will take more than yer words to win her affection."

"Mum." Callen's cheeks warmed. "She is still in too much pain—"

"Even more than physical love, Callen. She's had her heart broken. Ye need to be patient with her. Find what will touch her heart to the point of mendin' that shattered part of her. Then she will love ye as that great eagle did. He brought ye hares and small game for summers after ye released him. Do this right and ye'll win that bonny bride's affection just the same."

"What do ye suggest?"

Mum smiled, shrugged one shoulder, and turned for the hall. "That, ye'll have to discover on yer own, son. We women are a fickle breed.

What one cherishes, another disdains." Mum's words trailed behind her as she slipped inside.

Where did one begin wooing a woman he'd already wed?

"Good eve, Ina." Callen took her left hand in his and kissed it. "In me haste to claim ye as me wife, I fear I neglected somethin' rather important."

Her pale eyes considered him. Mum was right. Fear consumed her. The bit of lip she pinched between her teeth, the pulling together of her brows, and the tension in her hands exuded fear.

He smiled to reassure her as he slid a ring on her third finger.

A breath eased from her and she relaxed as she looked at it.

"It was me grannie's. Mum saved it to give to me bride."

"Thank ye."

Well, he hadn't expected to win her over on the first try, but he had hoped for a little more. So, jewelry wasn't the way to Ina's heart. He'd search until it found what was.

Davina sat in the solar with Malcolm and Freya. The candlelight caught on the gem on her hand as she toyed with the ring that sloshed about her finger. The gold band had leaves carved into it on either side of the mounted stone and three round nubs engraved with flowers. Two were near the leaves and the last was opposite the stone. The smooth, oval, blue stone allowed light to dance inside it like a dark-colored window. She'd never owned jewelry before and she feared its large size would cause her to lose it.

"I'm so glad ye're wearin' Mum's ring." Freya said with a smile. "Da gave it to her when they were married. It had been his mum's before that."

Three generations old. Davina would die if she lost it. She glanced at the wool strands of their weaving. Perhaps she could wrap the back of the band with some to make it fit better. She closed her fist. It would be best not to wear it at all.

Callen strolled into the room. His broad grin greeted her. He bent to kiss the top of her head as he passed and poured himself a drink. "Anyone need a refill?"

"No." Malcolm's sharp tone caused Davina to glance up. "Callen, are you sure about leaving tomorrow? The weather—"

"Aye, Da. I've made arrangements." Callen's tone was tight.

Freya pursed her lips and narrowed her gaze at the two men.

"But the new filly—" Malcolm pressed.

"—is fine. The mare tends her well. The Gunn lands are closest and the coin will be welcome now. A lot can happen between the covering and the foaling." Callen stared into his drink and bit off each word.

Malcolm slid to the edge of his seat. He clipped his words and pointed his finger. "Ye need not lecture me on horse husbandry, lad. I taught ye everythin' ye know."

"Aye, ye taught me, Da, but not all I know." He threw back his head as he downed the last of the drink. "I leave at first light," he said as he stood. "Mark and Neil join me." He stepped beside his mother and kissed her cheek. "See ye in a few days." He stepped to Davina next and kissed her as he had his mother. Just a peck on the cheek. "I'll be back before ye know it, Ina."

She watched him leave. The hollow pit where her heart once lay ached.

"That bull-headed fool. Now is no time—"

"Malcolm." Freya's soft chastisement cut off his words.

"Forgive me, Davina," he said with a sigh. "I fear 'tis the least of what ye'll hear between me son and me."

Freya's gaze held Davina, though she spoke to her husband. "Ye are both pig-headed, to my way of seein' thin's. Both so set in provin' the other wrong ye can nay see the merit in what the other has to say." She huffed and swung her hard gaze to her husband. "He has a wife, Mal. And ye cut in low in front of her."

Malcolm slouched back in his chair. His glass clattered against the carved arm. "Forgive me, lass. Me wife—as always—is correct. I don't mean to undermine him in yer eyes."

Davina shook her head. She didn't think any differently of Callen after his row. All she saw was another man fleeing her presence. Like Fergus had done, Callen, too, avoided time with her. But with Callen it was worse. He didn't just lock himself in a room; he left the manse for another clan.

Davina stared again at the closed door her husband had hurried through. Clans seldom lived close to one another. The Gunns could have been a day or two's ride away.

She blinked but found no tears had formed. Perhaps she was beyond the pain of men abandoning her.

A hand covered hers and squeezed. Davina glanced down and raised her gaze to Freya. The older woman's warm touch added to her kind gaze and her words gentle. "It will only be a few days, lass. He does this for ye."

Her? That made no sense. Davina set aside her near full glass and pinched the bridge of her nose. A headache brewed behind her eyes.

"Do ye not favor our wine, lass?" Malcolm had stood to refill his glass.

Davina shook her head, but stopped so quick her neck twinged, which added to her growing discomfort. "'Tis fine, m'laird."

He took a deep draft and moved to stand behind his wife. "What did Fergus serve ye?"

A war waged inside her. The memories of the sweet mead and the people of Seycoll flooded her, as did Fergus' betrayal and her longing to be back there again. "A berry mead," she said without a tremor in her words.

"Hmm." He tipped his head as his gazed searched about. "I believe we have some plum mead in the cellar."

While still holding Davina's hand, Freya took her husband's as she smiled at him. "Thank ye, Mal." She glanced at Davina again. "We'll make sure there is some here in the solar for you and some for the meals."

"I don't mean to be a bother. I—"

Freya squeezed her hand again. "Ye're family, lass. We want ye to feel at home here."

Home. The word set at odds within her. Home was lost to her, with no hope of ever recovering it again.

Chapter 38

Callen had left as planned with three of his stallions and headed to Gunn lands.

He played the moment in the solar over again in his head. Ina hadn't begged him to stay. Hadn't asked after what he did. She stared at him. Then Da had poked his nose in. The man treated him like a child. He had a wife now. As soon as Ina healed, he hoped to have barins of his own. Callen needed to build his own herd so he could provide for them. Why couldn't Da see that?

The journey to the neighboring clan had gone well, and the stallions took to their task with eagerness. But before Callen, Mark, and Neil could return home, a storm in the mountains between Gunn and Kincaid lands erupted. The passes filled with feet of snow. As days turned into a week and then over a fortnight, Callen fought the rage brewing inside him. Da's smug grin at being proved right on this ill-timed trip goaded him. But he knew better than to push the horses in the frigid weather. Most days, he paced in the Gunn hall, unable to eat, frantic to be on his way. His only thought was of Ina and what she must think of him.

"Cal, sit," Mark said.

"Aye, ye're making me dizzy." Neil munched on a bit of venison.

The two men could have been brothers. Mark was a year Callen's senior, and Neil two his junior, but both men wore their coal-colored hair the same length and kept their beards trimmed short. All three of them were second sons and in need of making a future for themselves. Their place in their families and their dreams of a good future bound them together.

Mark raised his cup in salute to someone at another table. "Cal, I don't know what yer all-fire hurry is. There are good people here." His eyes hooded and his lips curved in a lopsided grin.

Callen followed his friend's gaze to a bonny Gunn lass. Callen plopped down on the bench across the table from Mark, which blocked his line of sight. "I'm a married man."

"You sure about that?" Neil mumbled and licked his fingers clean. "If I was only a few weeks wed, I'd be spendin' all me days with me bride in our chambers." He elbowed Mark beside him. "Ye'd not see me, except for a meal now and then."

Callen narrowed his gaze. "She was sore injured when she arrived."

"Aye, we know." Mark groaned.

The two men said the next words together as though they had heard it told many times. "She almost died and ye didn't leave her side."

Neil picked up the tale, his hand flipping in the air as though he pointed to a thousand different places. "Until she was well, then ye spent all yer time in the stables or runnin' off across the country."

Callen sat his elbow on the table beside his plate and rested his chin on the heel of his hand. They didn't ken the torment of being with Ina, wed, but not able to touch her for fear of hurting her. In every way, he wanted to do as his friends suggested.

Did Ina think of his distance as his friends did? Did she think him uncaring and uninterested? He buried his aching head in his hands. The

Lord willing, Ina would be healed enough when at last they returned home and he could know his wife as he longed to.

Davina stood in the soggy yard of the Kincaid manse. Dressed in a coarse kirtle covered only in a filthy apron. She shivered.

"I'm so glad the snow stopped," the woman beside her said. She was closer to Freya's age with medium brown hair.

Davina hadn't bothered to learn the names of the people here. It would have been far easier to learn the names in Bothleigh. Unlike Seycoll, where most of the clan lived within the manse walls due to its location on the spit of land, here, only the laird's family and those who served his immediate needs lived within the walls. Most lived in the village outside the ground of Laird Malcolm's keep. Why did any of it matter? Her most recent husband had left near three weeks ago with few words. How long would it be before he sent her away, too?

A younger woman among them giggled. "Now that the snow has stopped, I bet the men will be returning." She flashed Davina a playful smirk. "I'm sure ye missed the fine laird's son."

"Oh, Sarah, I think it is ye who wish to see Mark just as much," another woman said.

The younger woman blushed as the others laughed.

The air was then rent with the horrid squeal of a pig. Another group of women, including Freya, pulled the poor creature as they brought it to where the other women waited. Davina closed her eyes and pressed her hand to her stomach as all the women worked to wrestle the large animal to the ground and someone slit its throat. Davina's stomach rolled in the silence left behind.

The women sped through their worked to gather the draining blood for black pudding along with its inners for sausage. They cut away fat for cooking grease, and they set aside hooves for jellies.

Davina did what she could to assist. She'd always enjoyed ham and bacon, but after watching the animal die and helping tear it apart while it was still warm, she wondered if she'd ever be able to eat it again.

The women looked up from the gruesome work at the sound of pounding hooves.

Callen had pressed their return home all day. His cheeks burned from the icy wind biting at them. Davina consumed his thoughts. He had to see her.

He charged through the gates of his home, leapt from his still moving mound, and tossed his reins to Gille, the groom in charge of his father's steeds. Davina wasn't in the hall, which wasn't surprising. She only came here for meals. No one answered at her chamber. He bound up the stairs to the solar. Where was she?

He returned to the yard and followed the cheerful chatter of women coming from the place where they slaughtered the hogs.

A woman with a flaming red braid knelt in the muck, helping to butcher the animal.

Callen released the breath caught in his aching lungs. "Davina."

She stood and turned as he approached. Her hand waved in front of her as she stepped back. "No!" She staggered back, caught her heel on the remains of the pig, and her arms pin-wheeled so he couldn't catch her before she plopped down in the waste with a *oof!*

He knelt beside her and tried to take her hands into his, but she refused. "Forgive me. I was eager to see ye, love."

"Oh?"

Her surprise hurt. "Aye, I missed ye."

She stood but remained out of his reach and her gaze fell on the rest of the women working to butcher the animal.

Mum stood and smiled at him. "We're glad to have ye home, Callen.

Ye go get the journey off ye and allow us to finish and clean as well. We shall meet ye in the solar in an hour."

Davina returned to her work without a backward glance. Had he lost her before he ever made her his?

Callen paced as he waited. Had the solar shrunk since last he'd been here?

Davina entered wearing a clean dress of green that made her hair stand out in contrast. "Ina." He took her hands, but she shied from him, so he only kissed her cheek.

Mum entered on her heels. "Did things go well for ye with the Gunn?"

Callen released Davina, and he followed the women to the chairs. "Everything went better than I ever hoped, but I'd have preferred to be here at Davina's side."

Her gaze narrowed on him, her brows pinched, and her head tipped. "Why?"

This was maddening. Callen wanted to yank her into his arms and kiss her until she understood his love was real.

Mum offered a knowing smile, rose, and left the room.

Callen came to crouch in front of Davina. He kissed the back of her hands, then the palms. "It is right for a man to miss his bride most dreadfully when they are apart."

"Oh."

Professing his undying love also was not the way to his love's heart. As she'd said before, words didn't always matter.

Chapter 39

Callen once again found his bride on the battlements, as he often did since his return from the Gunn a week ago. She stood in her leather cloak huddled against the chill wind. But inside or out, she seemed as closed off to him as she stood now. She spoke few words, unless she responded to a question he posed. So, he asked another. "Do ye prefer fox or rabbit?"

Davina turned from where she looked out over the southern valley. What did she search for? Was this some form of escape for her? "Excuse me?"

"Ye need a proper coat for our chilly winters. Would ye prefer it to be fox or rabbit?" Callen grin. He stepped closer to draw her into his arms but as she turned to face him, she stepped back.

"Neither, please. Their fur suits them far better than me. Me leather coat serves me fine for the short times I wander out of doors."

Callen drew near, rested his hand against the wall on either side of her. She remained rigid in front of him. "Is there nothing I can provide for ye, Ina?"

"Ye've provide a great deal. I'm warm, out of the harsh weather, and

I've plenty to eat. What more do I need?"

I don't know lass, but I'm trying to figure it out. "Might I stay and enjoy the view with you?"

She shrugged. "'Tis your manse. I'm sure you may go anywhere you wish." She turned and moved toward the door back inside. "I go to join your mother in the solar again."

Callen sighed as she walked away. Perhaps he should show her around their holdings? He thumped the top of the crenel with the side of his fist. But then, this wouldn't be their home once Dougal returned. He needed to search for a place in Kincaid lands where they would have a suitable home and land for raising horses. He sighed with a groan. Perhaps it was time to talk with Da.

Callen steeled himself, drew in a deep breath, and knocked on the cabinet door.

"Enter."

"Da, may I speak with ye?" He'd tried jewelry, a fine coat, a new pair of satin slippers to fit her petite feet while inside the keep. He offered the best of the meals and the finest wine. He'd even offered her the new filly born a fortnight ago. The promised mount had interested her for a moment, but she said she had only ridden twice and he could put the valuable animal to better use. Nothing drew Davina to him. Though he was loath to do so, he came to his da for help.

"Aye," Da waved him to a chair in front of the desk as he scoured a document. After a moment, Da scribbled a couple of notes and looked up. "Callen, how might I be of assistance?"

Why did Da assume he needed help? He was a grown man—married, no less. Callen was more than capable of handling his own affairs.

With a breath, he closed his eyes for a moment. It was stunning how fast his ire could rise in his father's presence. In truth, he had come for aid—it was that Da assumed he needed some that threatened to have him storm from the room without saying a word.

Callen gripped the arms of the chair and fought to keep his voice level and calm. "Might ye remember in yer brief time with Laird Fergus and Davina of anything she favored? I wish to aid her in adjusting to coming to our home."

Da sat back and stroked his beard. "Well, she spoke of her weaving. Fergus had bought her a wall loom, and she'd begun a tapestry. Perhaps in the spring ye can send for it so she might finish."

"She already weaves with Mum."

"Um, true. Have ye tried jewelry?"

"Aye, and furs, slippers, horses."

Da's hand dropped, and he focused on Callen. "I see. Is she unhappy?"

"Not that she'll say, but she seems—lost."

Da nodded and stood. Walking the few steps toward the window, he pulled the tapestry aside and opened a shutter for a moment. He rubbed his arms and returned to stand behind his chair. "I thought it wrong of Fergus to deceive her. I told him as much."

"Deceive her?"

"Aye, she never knew she was his ward. She believed the old man had wed her."

"I'd known she thought she was his wife, but didn't understand she believed so through trickery." Fergus' betrayal and the harsh treatment by her da lay at the root of her fear now with Callen.

"Aye. Fergus insisted it was for the best she believed, in the hopes it would keep Nathair at bay. Duncan said her pleas not to be sent away were heart-wrenching."

Is that why she stared out over the land? To see the place she'd left behind? Some days she stared out to the south, in the direction Seycoll lay. But as many times she looked on the loch north of Bottleigh. What did she search for?

"Books."

Callen clung to the arms of the chair to keep from bursting out of it at Da's sudden intrusion into his thoughts.

"Books?"

"She had just learned to read and was enjoying Fergus' collection."

Callen nodded as his gaze scanned Da's volumes along the right wall.

"She can come choose anything to her liking," Da said as he returned to his chair.

"Might be an enjoyable diversion over the next winter-bound months," Callen said with a nod. He drew in a deep breath and let it ease out. "There is one other matter, Da."

Setting his papers aside again, Da laced his fingers and smiled. "Of course."

"I wish to find a place to make our home. It would need land for the horses. The meadow near the Forklock rise is nice and near enough to our kin."

"Why do ye want to leave?"

"When Dougal returns—"

"Your brother would nay throw ye out of yer home, lad."

Callen stood. "Thank ye for suggestin' the books. I'll brin' Ina to pick some soon." He left the cabinet and stomped toward the stables. Any place outside the manse where others viewed him as a man, and not a child, would be preferable to here.

Callen spotted Da talking with some villagers who came to trade. Now would be a good time to offer Ina the access to the library. He slipped through the kitchen, crossed the hall, and bounded up the stairs two at a time. He entered the solar without knocking.

"Callen, love, what are you doing up here?"

He strolled to mother and kissed her cheek. "I hoped to borrow me bride for a moment?"

Ina looked up from her weaving for the first time.

He offered his hand, and she rose from the chair without taking it. As Ina moved toward the door, Mum nodded at him with encouragement.

"Callen, where are we going?" Davina's slow reluctant steps whispered behind him. He tried not to pull her down the stairs.

"I've something I hope will brighten yer day, love."

She slowed and would have stopped if he didn't hold her hand. "Ye provide me with too much. I don't require more."

"Even so." He opened the door to his da's empty study and brought her to the wall of books. "I thought ye might like to read something."

Her arms hung limp at her sides. No smile touched her lips. "That is very kind." There was no life in her words. Her finger ran along the spines on one shelf. Davina drew out two and cradled them in her arms. "Thank ye." Her gaze held his, but there was no connection between them.

He'd failed again.

CHAPTER 40

Callen leaned against the stable wall. Clouds hung low and dark on the horizon. Snow scented the air. With his eyes closed, he released a deep breath. Davina slipped further from his reach each day no matter what he did. *Lord, please.* He didn't know what else to say as his heart and mind churned like the approaching storm.

When he opened his eyes, Mum walked toward him and grinned in the way that told him she knew what was going on. "Mum, does she speak to ye? Do ye know what I might do?"

Mum caressed his cheek as she'd done when he was young. "She speaks very little, Callen. I worry over her. But remember yer eaglet. What did ye say to me? 'This wretched fowl can die for all I care. Dumb bird doesn't know what's good for it.'"

Callen stifled a groan. "But ye asked me to try one more time."

"And it took the meat then. Let ye pet it the next day. Don't give up now. She's worth the effort."

"Far more than a dumb bird," Callen added, knowing his mum would have said the same.

She offered him a discerning smile and continued about her day.

Callen spent the rest of the day preparing to take his stallions to the neighboring clan. After over a fortnight of trying to woo his bonny bride, he needed to focus on something he could accomplish. He had their future to consider. Strong stock would provide him a sizable cover fee from his stallions and hearty mares would grow his herd. Callen aimed to make his Highland ponies known throughout the entire land. Now he just prayed he still had a future with Ina too.

"I'm taking the stallions to the Macay's," Callen told Davina as the morning meal ended the next day. "The storm I thought might snow us in for a few days seems to have blown itself out."

She only nodded as she stared at the last bits on her plate.

"I'll return before the Lord's Day."

Again, she rewarded him with nothing more than a nod. *God, please show me soon the way to reach her.* Mum was right; she was growing quieter. He watched as she caught her breath when she stood. Her side still pained her. Shouldn't it be healed by now? Was it like her heart, in that it would never truly mend?

The weather had warmed and Callen returned a day early.

Da found him as he secured the horses in the stables. "How fared ye with the Macay?"

"Well." Callen shook the coin bag he'd collected.

"Received a missive today from the Keith's. They're interested in the same deal."

Callen paused and looked at Da. "Keith's? They be a traitorous lot. Why would they be seeking favors from the Kincaid?"

"Aye, there's long been bad blood between us. Could be an opportunity to form better relations." Da's voice held no hope for that, but neither did it carry disdain.

"Or for them to betray us and get me throat slit." Callen completed his tasks of seeing his animals settled.

Da nodded and walked with him toward the keep. "Aye. The choice is yers, of course. But thought I'd make ye aware."

Da left the decision to him with no goading toward his preference. That was a first. Callen stood a little taller and pushed back his shoulders. "After I see Davina, I'll give it some serious thought."

Da nodded and patted his shoulder before Callen left to search for his bride. After climbing the keep steps several times, he found her at last reading in the room where she'd bathed after her fever. She looked up. As though a common servant entered, she offered him no smile or other acknowledgement to his presence other than to glance at him.

He knelt before her and offered her a small dwarf cornel. "'Tis the first flower of spring, bloomed just for ye."

She took the delicate white flower and with care not to tear any of it, she spread the petals on a page in her book, then smashed it as she closed the covers.

Callen stood. "I thought ye'd like the wee bit of spring."

She looked up at him, face scrunched. "Have ye never given a lass a flower afore?"

"Aye, they most often put them in water and set them out to gaze at and enjoy."

"This isn't a rose. 'Tis a wee wildflower. Water won't keep it alive. Just plucking it made it wilt. But by pressing it between these pages, it will dry but not lose its color or even its sent. In a few days, I'll be able to remove it and enjoy it for far longer than any flower put in a vase."

He'd misunderstood. She'd wanted to save it, not destroy it. Could this be progress?

"Thank ye." She smoothed the cover of her book. "Ye've returned early. Did everything go well?"

"Aye, another successful trip and the weather was favorable. We should have a good herd of our own soon."

"You are gathering a herd?"

He took a seat beside her. "Aye. I'll have the best Highland Ponies in me stable. I'll provide well for ye."

She scrunched up her bonny features again as she stared at him.

Before she could speak again, Morag poked her head in. "M'lady," She spotted Callen and nodded to him. "And m'laird. The meal is ready."

Davina cradled the book close to her as she stood. Was she thinking of the flower? She set the tome in her chamber and took his arm and descended the stairs.

Before they stepped into the hall, he stopped and kissed her. Smelling of harebell and tasting sweet, she stirred his longing to be with her. But she startled at his touch as she always did. "I'm glad to be home and by yer side again, Ina."

She blinked and searched his face. Did she search for the truth of his words or something more?

Chapter 41

Davina donned her leather coat, draped her plaid over her head and shoulders, and ambled out onto the wall. Her mind recalled the love story she'd been reading. Would she ever know those emotions again?

Her eyes caught on the kirk. She hadn't been to prayers, other than on the Lord's Day. Even then, she said little to the Lord. She wouldn't say she was angry at God. That would be blasphemy. God was sovereign and could do as He pleased. Yet, she didn't ken how breaking her heart was part of His plan. But hers was not to question, she'd always been told. So, she didn't speak at all. But perchance she'd feel better if she met with God.

She watched her breath float away on the crisp breeze. What would it take to make her feel at home with Callen? How did she trust his words when he treated her little different than Fergus? Her fingertips brushed across her lips. Fergus never kissed her. No one had pressed their lips anywhere but her hands. The visiting lords had—

Fergus had business with each. Only Lord Malcom had agreed. Aye, Callen's father had agreed and was supposed to have returned to collect her on his way home.

Davina's breath caught. Fergus had been trying arranging her marriage with those men. He conspired to be rid of her right there on the dais during the meal and she never saw it. At least Crom hadn't hid that he offered for sale to the crowd. She'd known what he was doing and prepared herself for what was to come. Fergus had plotted to do the same behind her back.

She blinked back tears as Callen came to mind—as he so often did. He was an admirable man. Unlike Fergus, he sought her out and didn't avoid her. He gave her presents. Despite that, she wasn't his wife. Not in any of the ways that mattered.

Callen spent much of his time with the horses. They seemed to be his responsibility, and he said the herd he was building would provide for them. Davina didn't ken why the manse wouldn't provide what they needed. But the horses were important to him. Perhaps one day he'd share them with her. Teach her to ride and take her with him on his travels. He'd offered her a filly several weeks ago. But she was little and it would be some time before Davina would be able to ride her.

Davina looked out over the tree-covered land. They might one day ride all the way to the sea. She wondered how far the waves were from Bottleigh. She released a long sigh. Did it matter? Did anything matter when they her treated little more than a guest in her own home?

The bright crisp morning marked almost two months since Davina and Callen had exchanged consents in the kirk. Yet he was no closer to figuring out how to woo her. She stood atop the walls as she so often did. He almost turned and headed to the stables. At least the horses would be happy to see him.

Mum passed him. She smirked her knowing smile and continued without a word.

Aye, Mum. I'll keep trying.

Callen climbed the steps, but he had no words for her today. He stepped up from behind, slipped his arms around her, and rested his forehead against the back of her head.

His wife was stiff, cold, unbending.

Lord, please.

He remained a few moments longer and decided the stables would be a far more welcoming place. Just as he was about to release her, the breath she'd been holding eased into the air in a misty cloud. Her muscles relaxed, and she settled her weight against him.

Callen tightened his grip and waited. Had he at last found the way to Ina's heart? It seemed too easy.

Callen held her. Oh, he'd cradled her head before, kissed her senseless and carried her up and down the stairs in the beginning, out of necessity. But now he wrapped his arms around her for no other reason than to hold her. His firm embrace surrounded her while it yet remained tender.

How many times had her heart pleaded for Fergus to hold her like this?

Her head lulled back and rested under his chin. Then she covered his hands with her own.

She fit against him so well.

Callen pressed his lips to the top of her head and released a long breath. "That I could stay here and never let ye go."

She pulled from him and turned, and he regretted opening his mouth. Tears teetered on her lashes, and desperation filled her gaze. "Do ye mean that?"

Did he? Would he allow her to remain in his arms? Why did being held bring such grateful tears to her eyes?

Da had only touched her with a cruelity.

Fergus only her hand.

But Callen …

Callen spread his arms and waited.

She searched his face.

"Forever."

She didn't step as much as she leaned forward. Her arms tucked between them as she, again, eased into his embrace. Every part of her was soft against him. Her head lay on his shoulder and her hand came to rest over his pounding heart. He stroked her back.

This was what her heart cried out for. More than words, to be held when everyone else had shunned her touch. To be surrounded by strong loving arms … to feel his heart beat against her … Here she might find home again.

Davina remained in his arms. Every inch of her flesh came alive and warmed. Yes, if she stayed in his embrace forever, it would be enough. To know that someone cared more than with words, but to embrace her. "Thank ye." The words were heavy with tears.

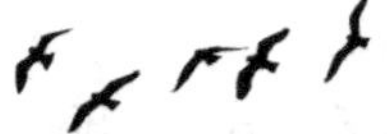

Callen dared to raise her chin to look at her. Light sparkled in her eyes and it was more than the tears. "I love ye." He pressed a kiss to her lips and for the first time, she answered. Her hand moved from his heart to the back of his neck to pull him closer. A hint of mead remained on her lips, and that combined with her heated kiss, was a heady combination.

He pulled from her lips with regret, but she rewarded him with a little merriment playing on her lips. Her arms encircled him and her head again slipped beneath his chin. Her heart beat against his chest as she clung to him.

True to his word, Callen continued to hold her.

She was the one to draw from his embrace. She rose on her toes and kissed him. "Thank ye, Callen." Her plaid swayed as she walked away, her steps bright.

When Morag poked her head in the solar to announce midday, Davina secured her bobbins and stood with Freya.

"Ye're almost finished with another plaid. What does that make now, four?"

"Five, I think," Davina said as they moved down the stairs.

"I don't think I know anyone who can weave as fast as you, my dear." Freya stopped on the landing near Davina's room. "I think I heard you humming today." Callen's mum offered her a lop-sided smile. "It is good to see you happy, Davina."

Something changed in those long moments cradled in Callen's arms. She found herself again. No, she'd found who she always wanted. Another human being who didn't just say they wanted her near, but who held her tight. Callen had corralled her errant emotions and penned them in until she more than saw or heard his love. She felt it deep in her weary soul. It was such a simple thing. No one would think it of any account. But to be held as he had done meant the world to her.

As Davina and Freya completed their journey to the bottom of the stairs, Freya stepped around Callen, who waited. As his mother disappeared into the hall, her husband turned to her and opened his arms again.

Davina's heart fluttered, and she slid into his embrace with a long sigh. What was it about the tender touch of another? Why did this fortify her heart so?

Callen kissed the top of her head. "While I'd be keen on stayin' right here, I imagine someone will notice our absence if we don't join Mum and Da at the table."

She held to him for another moment. Not ready to let go.

"I promise, 'twill not be the last time I hold ye, love."

She nodded and drew from his warm embrace, swiped at a tear slipping down her cheek, and took his arm as he led her to her seat.

They ate with few words between them, but the warmth from his touch still consumed her. It awakened more than her heart. "Might I have a little more venison?"

Callen grinned as he picked up the tray and placed another large slice on her plate. "It does my heart good to see you eating, Ina."

She returned his smile. He was so good to her. She had seen it before, but as though through a thick fog. Somehow his embrace had cleared her view and her perception—not just of Callen, but of her surroundings. The food tasted better; the mead more sweet; the laughter of the kin at the table below more joyful, and their joy added to her own instead of bringing light to her lack. As though a culminating piece in a great work of art, now all that Callen had been doing for her seeped inside and proved his love was true as he'd said it was.

Each time Callen came near, he embraced her. Each day, a little more joy surfaced. There was something about being held in his arms that let her believe anything was possible. The morose fog that had consumed her lifted under his shining care. Callen was not like Fergus, nor Da. She believed him when he said he loved her. It took time, but her shattered heart mended and squeezed back together with each powerful embrace.

"Ah, Ina." His arms engulfed her and pulled her close. "I'm going to take the filly for some training."

Did she dare ask? What would become of these budding emotions if he refused her? She looked up and her lip slipped between her teeth.

His hand caressed her face as his other arm remained snug around her. "What is it, love?"

If he said no, it would be the end of her. She didn't dare ask.

His gaze searched her. "Do ye want to come with me?"

Tears bubbled, but she only nodded.

He pulled her close and kissed the top of her head. "I would like nothing more."

Again, she relaxed against him. He'd said yes. Perhaps he did want her for more than just a wife in name only.

"Ye go pick yer mount and I'll fetch some lads to join us."

She cocked her head, but he was already moving to the stairs. She ambled the other direction and down to the stables.

"Gille?" She peered into the dark stables. "Gille? Laird Callen and I are going for a ride." She stepped inside when she didn't hear a response. "Gille, are ye here?"

The horses pawed the ground, snorted, and tossed their heads.

A familiar stench hit her nose.

An arm clamped around her ribs and a hand slammed over her mouth. A harsh whisper ground into her ear. "Here I came to assure I'd get hold of the arse who thought he could steal from me Da, and the whore he stole walks right into me hands."

Chapter 42

Davina couldn't breathe, for another reason than that Nathair had her in his grasp. He covered her nose and mouth with his huge gloved hand.

"If I knew ye'd welcome anyone to yer bed, yer time in Seycoll would have ended so much more pleasant."

Why? Just when she had convinced herself to open her heart to Callen, why did Nathair return to destroy everything?

He turned her toward the door. "God has blessed me that I might punish ye for ruinin' me life."

Did God reward him and punish her? What had she done so wrong? The thought stuck in her like a fishbone swallowed the wrong way. God was love and what He had created between her and Callen was a gift. There lay the truth. Nathair lied.

"I'll teach ye how whores are to be treated and see if the thief still wants ye."

A fire burned in her. She'd not make her capture easy for him. A fortnight ago, she'd have let Nathair do his worst and never lifted a finger against him. But Callen loved her. And she loved him. She'd done nothing wrong. Fergus' deception caused his son to act out against her.

Her legs were already weakening from the lack of air. Davina went limp. She would not let her abduction be easy.

Nathair had just moved when she collapsed in his arms. He staggered and fought to keep his hold on her and his balance.

But his hand shifted, freeing her nose, and she drew in a deep breath. A finger fell between her teeth and she bit down on it like a starved dog on the last bone. She tasted leather and then blood before Nathair roared in her ear.

He jerked his hand away with a curse.

"CAL-LEN!"

Nathair whirled her around and raised his fist.

Pain exploded across her face.

A terror-filled scream raced between the buildings and bounced off the walls. Callen ran for the stables before his next heartbeat. A hooded figure on a shabby mount charged for the gate. The skirts of Davina's gown flapped in the wind he stirred as she hung, draped over the villain's lap.

"Stop them!" Callen shouted.

The hooded figure had two accomplices, and they challenged the Kincaid guards. The cur carrying Davina charged through the gate unhindered. Swords rang out as Callen switched directions and veered into the stables. He threw a harness over his favorite mount as five men from Bottleigh charged in to join him.

He tried to lead the stallion from his stall, but the mighty horse refused to set his right hoof down. The mount's refusal forced Callen to stop and check. A shard of metal protruded from the soft center.

"Check their feet," he instructed the others.

He'd planned to take this horse to the Keith's on the morrow. Callen glanced out the stable doors toward the empty gate. What had that man been up to when Davina entered? And were the Keith's behind it?

"Gille!"

Callen turned as someone bent over the groom's prone body. "Is he alive?" Callen and two others asked.

"Aye," Neil answered.

One guard from the gate stumbled in, holding his bloody arm. "Forgive us m'laird. We failed to stop him." He looked down at Gille. "We'll take care of him. Get after her before they get too far."

Callen saddled a different mount and swung up, only to pause before spurring his horse to speed.

The bloody guard stood in his path and looked at him. "It was Nathair."

"Ha!" Callen kicked his horse hard and flew across the courtyard and out the gate.

"To the south!" someone called from atop the wall.

Neil and the others charged behind him. None of them spoke. They all knew the danger Davina was in if Nathair had her.

The throbbing in Davina's head intensified at being slung over someone's lap as they galloped across the countryside. But she didn't move. The sun warmed her back as she waited. She hung limp and tried not to groan.

"Ye have the prize ye sought. Let's enjoy her and get out of here," a voice beside her said.

"No. We wait for Seycoll. They'll all know the woman she truly be," Nathair said.

She was on his horse; sprawled across his lap. At least she had time to find an escape. She wasn't able to fight off two men. But her head ached from the blood flooding it in her current position. Her stomach pained her almost as much as when he'd stabbed her as it took the brunt of the pounding from the frantic escape. She just needed a little of God's favor to slip away. Callen wouldn't be far behind.

"Ye know they won't let ye do naught to her. Best kill her and flee to England." That voice differed from the first's and not Nathair's

Davina stifled a shudder. At least two others rode with him. The bouncing grew intolerable. Her fingers tingled as they dangled above her head and her chin and nose kept hitting his leg. Though unbound, she couldn't escape him at this speed.

Lord, help.

Moments later, the air cooled and the light dimmed. Hooves crunched through leaf litter and they slowed.

"We'll lose them in the trees. They won't be able to follow at speed," Nathair said.

Davina breathed easier for a few minutes, listening, waiting. When the sound of the other horses seemed fainter, she pushed off with her numb arms and slid to the ground.

Her foot landed on a rock. Her ankle buckled, and a crack filled the air over Nathair's curses. She fell back, unable to carry weight on the injured limb. Fabric rent as her shoulder scraped against rough bark.

Stunned, it took her a moment to climb to her feet. Her injured leg wouldn't bear any weight.

Nathair seized her by her plait and yanked her head back. He spun her around and the back of his hand crashed into her face. Fairy light danced among the shadows.

"Let me go!" Her loud shout add to the ache in her head and made her words thunder inside her skull.

"Shut her up," one of the others said.

"CAL-LEN!" She screamed with all her might as Nathair tore a strip of her skirt away. She tried to kick him, but the impact hurt too much to be effective.

She slapped his hands away. "They are going to kill ye when they come." Once again, she cried out her husband's name.

Nathair grabbed the base of her plait once more, spun her, and jerked her close. His filthy arm draped over her shoulder. His breath held the scent of death. "Not before I'm done with ye."

His fermented breath soured her stomach. "They come. Run while ye can." She thrust her arms against his chest and twisted from his grasp, but with her injured leg, she lost hope of getting away from him.

One of the other men circled around them. "She's right. They follow close. Get her under control or leave her."

"CALLEN!" Her shriek echoed through the near bare branches.

Wham. His hand crashed into her face again and she crumpled to the ground rather than fall backward.

Nathair forced a strip of fabric between her teeth and tied it behind her head, along with several loose strands of hair, doubling the ache in her skull. She clawed at it until he captured both her hands and tied them behind her back.

She threw her head back into him but missed.

"Ye'll pay for each injury ye inflict on me and for every moment ye delay the inevitable." He pulled her to her feet by her hair and a cry of pain vanished in the gag.

He mounted, and she spun out of his reach. Hopping on one foot, she maneuvered into a narrow space between two broad trunks. The low branches kept his horse from getting close.

She scraped her face against the bark to dislodge the gag. "CAL—"

Nathair's hand slammed over her mouth, splitting her lip and caused metal washed over her tongue. His other hand clamped around her throat, cutting off her air. "Shut up or I'll toss yer dead body and that of yer lover's at me father's feet."

Chapter 43

Forced to dismount when the light failed, Callen led his horse through the thick forest. He'd be no good to Davina knocked unconscious by a low-hanging branch or if something injured his mount in the dark. He was sure he'd heard her scream. But it was hard to discern over the pounding of his heart. He couldn't lose her. Not now.

"We should stop," one man said.

"Ye can, if ye wish. I'll not cease until I have me wife."

"Sounds like a stream on our right. Let's at least water the animals," Neil said.

Callen relented. The horses would be key to running Nathair to ground.

As the horses waded into the water and drank their fill, Mark came beside him. "They take her toward Seycoll."

"It would appear so, though Nathair is capable of great deceit." Callen shook his head.

Mark held his gaze and spoke the words lodged as a lump in Callen's throat. "I pray we catch them before he inflicts whatever damage he intends."

Neil approached. "Rodger returned to get a skiff and sail south to alert Fergus. We'll trap him between us and end him."

"He's mine." Callen jerked his horse's reins and stomped into the darkness.

"We have to stop or be killed," one of Nathair's men said.

"They are only a breath behind us. We stop and we will be dead." The other man turned to Nathair. "Can't ye hear them crashing through the trees in our wake as well as I."

Nathair swore at the man. "The trees will thin soon. McKenzie lands lay open and will be easy to cross, even in little moonlight."

"Easy for them that chase us as well," Nathair's man grumbled.

Davina sat across Nathair's lap. Her injured ankle often banged into her other leg, and it had swollen, making her toes tingle in her boot. The pain brought unwanted tears. His arm remained locked around her ribs —when his hand wasn't roaming higher to grope her. She fought to draw a breath. Her head throbbed, and she wanted to sleep, but the constant jostling and pain kept slumber far from her.

In desperation, she kicked their horse's shoulder at the same time as she jerked around in his grasp and hit his nose with her head.

"Ye filthy wench."

She screamed at him through her gag.

Nathair swiped the blood away and grabbed a fistful of hair. She cried out again.

"She slows our escape. Leave her." The man on his right veered off into the trees.

"Not till I have me revenge. Me own kin turned against me as their rightful ruler in favor of her. They will bear witness to what I will do to each one who has betrayed me. They will know the fear of my name."

The other man followed the first with a snort. "Will be the death of us all."

"So be it!" Nathair said.

The kiss of salt in the air roused Davina from her headache-killing, faint sleep. They'd raced through the night and much of the day. Bouncing on the charging horse, clutched in Nathair's grasp, her leg throbbed. She just wanted to stop moving. Then she captured salt air with what little air she could draw into her lungs.

They cleared the last of the trees, the afternoon light glinted off Seycoll as it sat perched atop its near island. She closed her eyes for a moment, finding the crash of the waves under pounding hooves. Gannet and corncrake bid her welcome. She opened her eyes and gazed at the only place that had ever felt like home. She had half a mind to thank Nathair.

He reined in and pushed her off his lap. Her good leg took most of the impact, but her injured ankle hit the ground and she pitched forward. With her arms still bound behind her, she twisted to land on her shoulder. Her head slammed into the only hard bit of land anywhere around her.

When she woke again, her hands were bound before her, and Nathair stretched them over her head. She tried to fight him, but she didn't have the strength, even on a good day. He drove a stake into a loop of her bindings, which secured her to the ground. She lay in full view of the manse.

"When they see, they'll hate ye." Spittle dripped on her face from Nathair's words.

Davina rubbed her face against her arm until she dislodged the gag. She laughed at him, though it hurt her head and bruised ribs. "Ye are the biggest fool if ye think one thing ye do to me will do anything but provoke them to hate ye all the more."

Her gaze shifted back to her beloved walls. The gates stood open and men on charging horses streamed out. Others lined the wall. "Look. Even now they come to stop ye."

"Nathair, we must leave." His companions wheeled their mounts and fled back into the trees.

"They'll not find ye alive." Nathair sat over her and drew his sword.

The ground thundered with charging hooves. Movement drew her gaze from the sword rising above her heart. Callen charged over the hill toward her. *'I love ye,'* she mouthed.

"Nathair!" Callen roared.

Nathair seized her chin, jerked her face to look at him, and slammed her head into the ground. "The last thing ye'll see is me."

She couldn't see much of anything as a dark fog narrowed her vision to a small tunnel.

The flash of metal hovered above her, but he'd released her to hold it with both hands. He blocked her view of Seycoll, so she turned again to Callen. He was only mere yards away, but too far to stop the sword from plunging into her.

She let her eyes close, welcoming the dark. Regret filled her to know that she'd never be the wife of the one man who'd truly loved her.

Davina lay beneath Nathair's sword. Too far away. Callen pushed his horse to its limit. It could move no faster. *Lord, please.*

Nathair stopped and glanced down at his chest. An arrow had pierced him. A second slammed through him.

Callen continued to race toward them; his horse churning up the turf.

Nathair's head dropped until his chin touched his collar. His arms fell to his side and his sword dropped only a breath from Davina.

Callen was only mere strides away as Nathair's slain body pitched forward. The deadly arrow tips headed for Davina.

Please, Callen pleaded. He reached them and kicked Nathair's lifeless body off her as he reined in, his horse's hooves only inches from her. He dropped to the ground and worked to free her.

"Take her inside. We'll run these others to ground," a man from Seycoll shouted as he charged past.

Davina lay still, splattered by Nathair's blood, with welts on her face, and a split lip. But the worse was he couldn't wake her. Cradling her head to his chest, he found a large lump on the side.

"Let me hold her while ye mount." Mark knelt beside them.

It would only be for a moment, but he didn't want to relinquish her. Callen caressed her face.

"The faster ye get her within Seycoll, the sooner a doctor can treat her injuries."

Callen relented and let Mark pick her up as he regained his saddle. Once she was snug in his arms, Callen turned them toward the manse and moved as fast as his exhausted horse and his wounded bride could tolerate.

Several of Fullarton's kin waved him toward the hall and took his reins.

"Bring her this way."

"The physician awaits to tend her wounds."

"Come."

He climbed the narrow stairs to the third floor behind a young maid. "Here m'laird." She pushed open a door of a large bedchamber.

A thin man in a white apron waited beside the bed. "Lay her here."

Callen held her close, scrutinizing him.

"He is Luke, our physician, Laird Callen." An older man stood at an open door in the side of her chamber that led to another room. "Luke will give her the very best care. And ye can come with me."

Callen laid her down on the bed stripped of its ornate bedcoverings. "I'll not leave her."

"Give us a wee bit to get her all cleaned up and tended to. We'll take right fine care of her. We will." A plump, middle-age maid shooed him from the side of the bed and she and Luke tended Davina's wounds.

"Please, Laird Callen. Fergus would speak to ye. There isn't much time left." The older man led him into the other chamber.

Callen watched Davina with every step. "Take good care of her."

The plump maid swiped an annoyed wave at him. "Like we'd do anythin' else," she said with a snort.

Chapter 44

The withered man propped against the pillow didn't resemble the powerful laird Callen remembered visiting with Da when he was younger. Fergus' skin was almost as gray as the last whisps of hair clinging to his head. His cheekbones jutted out like boulders along the coast. And his sunken eyes peered out of his wrinkled face.

Those eyes turned on him now. The laird's voice rattled. "Is she …?"

"Yer Luke attends her. She has a lump on her head and marks on her face from a beating."

"That worthless wretch. I should have ended him long before she arrived." Again, Fergus' weak gaze fell on Callen. "He didn't …?"

Callen didn't know the answer, feared it, in fact. But he clung to one hope. "We didn't give him time to slow. Pressed his movement all night."

Fergus dropped back into the pillows and remained still. Callen wondered if he'd gone to the other side, but Fergus patted the side of his bed. "Come, lad. Let me tell ye everythin'."

"Laird Fergus is gone," Owen said as he followed Callen back into Davina's chamber.

She lay covered in a clean sleeping garment. Her right wrist and left ankle were both splinted.

Luke wiped his hands on one of the bloody sheets piled on the floor. "I'll see he is prepared for burial."

The maid crossed herself. "The Lord, bless him." She dipped a curtsy to Callen and nodded to Owen. "The lasses will scrub the chamber clean, create a new mattress, and replace the beddin'."

Callen stopped Luke as he headed toward Fergus' chamber. "Doctor?"

"She still sleeps, which could speak to her harrowing night as much as to the injuries to her head."

Callen again looked at the bloody sheets.

"Her ankle suffered a severe break. While her boot kept the broken bones still for the most part, avoiding further injury, it also caused swelling that did damage to the muscle. I had to drain some blood to relieve the pressure. Only time will tell if she received treatment in time to save the leg."

Callen seized the bedpost to keep from collapsing. "When should she wake?"

"I'll check on her in a half an hour. God be willin', I won't need to bore into her skull to remove any pressure there. If the Lord wills it, and there is no further treatment required, I'd hope to see her awake by mornin'."

Callen nodded, still relying on the bedpost to keep him upright. "Thank ye."

Luke nodded. "She'll suffer headaches and dizzy spells for weeks to come." He nodded toward the maid. "And light and sound will pain her too."

The maid shuttered the windows, leaving only the flickering candle beside Davina's bed to light the room. Luke and Owen left.

"I'll stay with her." Callen moved to sit on the bed with Davina.

"Might ye do me a boon and fetch me a wee bit to eat and something to drink?"

"I can watch her, m'laird. I can."

Callen rested a tender hand on the maid's arm. "I know. But I can't bear to be parted from her just now. Would ye be a dear?"

She inclined her head with a bit of an irritated smirk, but did as he requested.

Alone with his bride, he almost groaned as he caressed her face. He was right back where he'd been months ago; sitting vigil beside his injured love.

He closed his eyes. "Thank Ye, Lord. The foul creature did not kill her, and he will suffer in the pit for all eternity. Let Ina's healing not take as long this time. I have a powerful need for me wife, Lord. Please."

"Amen. And amen." The maid stood beside the bed with his tray of food.

A relentless throb filled her head, and it had a pounding echo. Saint's, she hurt.

But she could breathe with ease now. And she'd stop moving. Where was Nathair, and what was he up to?

She searched her muddled thoughts with trepidation as even thinking hurt. She still smelled Seycoll's salt air. The gentle crash of the waves teased her, but they were somehow far too loud. Oh, this pounding was unbearable.

She tried to shift. Pain raced down her spine, halting any further attempts, and something tightened around her. Was she still in Nathair's control? Foggy images of him sitting atop her, ready to plunge a sword into her, floated back. Clearly, he'd failed. Though the drumming in her head made her almost wish he'd succeeded.

Her wrists and legs were bound. No, just one wrist and one leg.

Hadn't she hurt her ankle?

Was that a gannet's call? Oh, heaven help her, but she needed to move. She stirred again and wiggled anything but her head. The band tightened around her again and then it stroked her arm. The thumping echo increased its tempo.

She pried one eye open and squinted against the single flame. She lay snuggled under the bedcovers, resting her head against Callen's chest as he sat atop them. He caressed her cheek. She tried to tip her head to look at his face, but it stirred a wave of unease to roll in her stomach like a skiff tossed in a storm.

"Oh, lass. I've half a mind to seal ye in this chamber and never let ye venture out where ye might get hurt again. Twice now, ye've near scared me into an early grave."

Though she couldn't look up at him, her gaze swept over her surroundings. "We're in Seycoll?"

"Aye, love. Yer home."

Home. What did that mean? Callen was returning her to Fergus? He didn't want her anymore?

She clutched at his rumpled, dirty tunic and tried to pull herself up. The splint on her wrist prevented her from getting a good hold on him, and she lay on her other arm.

"Callen, please. Don't leave me. Nathair didn't do what he intended. I'm yers. Please."

Chapter 45

The movement and pleading with Callen not to leave her blinded her with pain. Her stomach rolled, and she feared she would wretch on him. "Please, don't leave m—"

Callen slid down to lie beside her and stopped her words with a tender kiss. He pried her fingers from his shirt and laced them with his. After a moment, he released her mouth and offered her a mischievous grin. "Forgive me, Ina, for not being more clear. *We* are home."

"We? You want to live here with Fergus?"

He brushed hair from her face. "Nay, love. Fergus has gone. They prepare him for burial. His last act was to save ye for Nathair and end the fiend."

"They're both dead." Sorrow and relief warred within her. "How is it Seycoll is now our home?"

Callen's finger traced a pattern on the back of her hand. "Ol' Fergus' loved for ye ran deep. Perhaps as strong as I." He smiled and kissed the tip of her nose. "After Nathair attacked Rachel, Fergus sent word to the king that he denounced his son and claimed ye as heir, informin' the king that Fergus intended to leave Seycoll to ye."

So her head might be more injured than she first realized. "But women can't inherit land and titles—especially when they aren't blood."

"A few have done it before. The king allows women to hold the land in their name until they choose a man to marry."

"I choose ye."

A kiss brushed her bruised cheek. "Oh, how I love ye."

"And ye."

He cradled her cheek and stared. Did tears pool on his lids?

A thought tumbled in her aching head. "What happens when they marry?"

Callen smirked. "By law, the husbands own the land after that, but the woman still holds a measure of power and say over what can happen to it."

Davina fought to make sense of the news. "So, we be staying here?"

"If that is what ye wish."

"But what of Bottleigh?"

He pulled from her a little and stared. "What of it?"

"What will yer da say when ye choose to remain here and not take the lands of yer birth?"

Callen stared at her for a moment. "Lass, they were never mine to have."

Davina closed her eyes but didn't dare shake her head. "I don't understand."

"I'm the second son. Dougal, my brother, is the eldest. Bottleigh goes to him. Why did ye think I was buildin' a stable of fine horses?"

She glanced at him with a shrug. "I couldn't figure it out."

He laughed and she winced at the joyous sound. He kissed her forehead. "Forgive me, lass, but why didn't ye ask?"

"I figured if ye wanted me to know, ye'd say."

"Ye are now lady of this grand holdin', m'love. Ye'll need to ask questions if ye want to be efficient in runnin' it."

She relaxed and let her head rest on his arm. "Can ye be happy here?"

He kissed her forehead again. "I never dreamed of holdin' such a property. 'Tis far grander than Bottleigh, and it holds a powerful place on the coast for defense. Bein' at Seycoll with ye will outshine me da and me brother. I'm overwhelmed with the blessin' of bein' yer husband, Ina." He drew her closer. "Now, stop yer frettin' and sleep, lass."

She closed her eyes and drew in a deep, salt-laced breath. It added to his musky spice that reminded her of the horses Callen raised. "What of yer herd?"

"Rest Ina, we'll discuss all later."

"Callen?"

He sighed. "Aye, lass."

Her fingers brushed over his beard and across his cheek. "I do love ye. Forgive me for not trusting ye sooner."

He kissed her fingers. "There is nothin' to forgive. I ken the hurt and betrayal ye felt. Fergus begged me to seek yer forgiveness for his actions."

She eased herself to nestle against him. "Fergus gave me to ye. How can I not be grateful to him?"

Chapter 46

Davina jerked awake, clutching at Callen's departing warmth.

"Shh, love." He kissed her hand as she fought to open her eyes. "I'll be back in a short while. We go to lay Fergus to rest."

She forced herself up on one elbow, but the movement renewed her headache and the room tilted. "Has the wake ended already?"

"Fergus had no remainin' kin save those within these walls. He didn't, m'lady."

Davina did her best to make a slow turn to look at Izbeil. Still, the dizziness blurred her vision and fouled her stomach. "Did Fergus not think me his daughter?"

"Aye, love."

She turned back to Callen and squeezed her eyes closed, hoping the room would stop pitching as if it was tossed about by a wild sea. "I've not said me farewells."

"Ina, yer too …"

"He asked for me forgiveness. His soul needs rest and I'll offer me words." She struggled to sit up.

"Now, m'lady …"

"I'm getting out of this bed and going down to the wake. Ye can help me or nay, but, by the saints, I shall find a way down those winding stairs."

Izbeil's fists perched on her hips. "What did ye do to her, m'laird?"

Callen gasped. "What did *I* do to her?"

"Aye, she sounds like a proper, willful, demandin' lady of the manse. Bullheaded, I say."

"I didn't demand ye do anything," Davina sputtered. Saints, her head hurt.

Callen came around the bed and eased her to her feet. "I think Izbeil offered ye a compliment, love."

He held her still as her forehead pressed into his chest. "I didn't demand."

He kissed her head and chuckled. "But ye were forceful in yer wishes."

She kept her head pressed against her husband, though she turned to look at the maid. "'Tis the *proper* thing to do, right Izbeil?"

The maid waved a dismissive hand at her. "We shall do as ye wish, m'lady." She opened the wardrobe.

"Something simple, Izbeil. The green gown I arrived in would be fitting."

"Nay." She wrinkled her nose. "I've thrown that rag out."

"Izbeil!" Davina regretted the sharp bark. She closed her eyes again and clung to Callen.

"Ye are the Lady of Seycoll proper now. Ye must dress to yer station at all times." She pulled out a deep blue satin gown and returned to the bedside. "This was the frock Fergus always preferred."

"I'll leave ye to it. I've need to change me own wrinkled tunic." Callen made sure Izbeil had her steady before slipping next door.

"By the sword!"

Davina gazed into the mirror to see Callen standing slack-jawed behind her.

"Ye are vision, Ina. Fergus was right."

Izbeil finished the loose, simple plait. "'Tis not a proper hair style for the lady."

"Izbeil, my head throbs just rising it off the pillow. It was near intolerable to allow ye to do what ye did. No more, please."

Izbeil snorted her disapproval.

A knock sounded at Callen's door. He opened Davina's and waved the caller down. "Aye?"

Owen stepped into view. "We are ready for ye, m'laird."

"Lady Davina wishes to say her farewells."

Owen nodded with a quick grin to her. "Very well. I shall inform the others of the delay."

"We will be down in a few moments," Callen said.

Owen inclined his head again and disappeared.

Callen moved to stand behind her and met her gaze in the mirror. "Ready, love?"

She reached out her hand, and he gathered her up and cradled her close. His steady beating heart comforted her and his warmth eased her tight muscles.

Chapter 47

Davina nestled into Callen's arms and closed her eyes as they wound down the stairs.

"Love?"

She looked up at him with a smile. Winding her fingers into his hair, she pulled him down for a kiss.

He chuckled. "Thank ye, lass, but can ye point me in the correct direction?" Davina hadn't realized they'd stopped at the bottom of the stairs. He turned them to the left.

"There lies yer cabinet."

"I have a cabinet." His muscles relaxed as the words sighed into the air.

"Aye." She managed a small giggle that didn't cause too much pain.

"I never thought to have a cabinet. Or even a small chamber from which to conduct me business."

"Did ye plan for us to live in a hovel with the horses on one side?"

He kissed her forehead. "Maybe a house and a stable." His happiness made her want to dance, but the thought of spinning around reawakened the nausea.

He turned them back in the other direction, and he carried her around the bend that led to the great hall. The joyful mutterings of the manse folk and lively music grew as they neared the wide opening into the expansive room. She glimpsed Owen and the room hushed. Benches grated against the stones beneath the reeds. Then there was no sound at all.

The wake had ceased. Everyone stood, not honoring Fergus—whose body lay in front of the dais—but looking at her. Matthew, Angus, Duncan, and Owen were in the front, shoulders squared and heads held high. Callen had only carried her a few steps into the room when the men in front took a knee and everyone behind them followed—men on one knee, the women and children on both.

They spoke. Their words jumbled at first, but soon they found a common rhythm and spoke as though only one. "I will be faithful and loyal and will maintain faith and fidelity to Lady Davina and to the husband she has chosen, Laird Callen, and to their heirs, in matters of life and limb and of earthly honor against all mortal men; and never will I bear arms for anyone against her or her laird or heirs. So may God help me and the Saints."

Her chest ached at the love they'd shown her, no matter how inappropriate it was to swear fidelity to a woman. Tears eased down her cheeks and she wiggled out of Callen's arms to stand on quaking legs before them. "It is kind and generous, and …" There were proper words to say in response and she wanted to honor them as they had revered her.

"And right that those who offer to us unbroken fidelity …" Callen whispered in her ear.

She repeated after him as he gave her each portion that followed. She spoke the words with a conviction she felt down to the soles of her feet. "… should be protected by our aid. And since such faithful ones of ours, by the favor of God, kneel here in our shared home, have seen fit to swear trust and fidelity to us, therefore we decree and command that for the future all these loving kin be counted with the number of Seycoll and the clans Fullarton, Kincaid, and Moffat. And if anyone perchance should presume to harm or kill any of them, let him know he'll be judged guilty and suffer severely."

Her kin—for that is what all of them were now—couldn't contain their joy as they stood to their feet. And Davina's tears wouldn't abate either. "Thank ye."

They bowed or curtsied, but didn't speak.

A shaggy head poked out between the adults. "We sore missed ya, m'lady."

Unable to find words, she waved Rory to her and kissed his head. "And I all of ye. I missed ye until me heart ached, but I shan't be leaving again."

"Hurrah!" The shout of everyone startled her back into Callen.

"We'd already planned to bar the gates to prevent ye escapin' again," Duncan said, and everyone laughed.

"After we bury the old laird, will ye come play shinty with us?" Rory said.

Davina raised her hem enough to show the lad her splinted ankle and bare toes. "It will be a wee bit afore I can join ye again. But I shall sit on the steps and watch."

There were disappointed groans scattered around the room.

She looked out on all these she loved. "Let me a wee mite to say me farewells, then ye men may attend to the burial."

They bowed and turned back to talk amongst themselves. Maids refilled cups and everyone piled their small trenchers full with the many available food items. Some women returned to their duties as Davina eased around and hobbled to Fergus.

He was so thin. Izbeil had said he suffered after he sent her away, but she hadn't dreamed it would show on his body so. She touched his cold arm, careful not to upset the plate of soil and salt perched on his still chest. They had honored their Laird with loam to show they would bury his body and return it to the earth whence it came. The salt represented his eternal soul.

"Thank ye, Fergus. And ye must forgive me for not kenning what ye were doing. Ye were so good and kind to me and I missed too much 'cause of yer silence. Ye did right by me in me father's stead." She reached out for Callen, who remained near. He stepped close and laced their fingers together. "Ye chose an excellent husband for me. He shall tend to Seycoll well and run it with honor and excellence. Thank ye, Da. Rest ye well, knowing I am loved and happier than I ever dared dream." She leaned down and kissed his cheek. It was an odd sensation, her lips touching his cold, lifeless skin.

Callen wrapped his arms around her and gave a little squeeze. "Thank ye, Laird Fergus, for entrustin' to me such a precious jewel. I shall love Davina and Seycoll until I draw me last breath, as ye did." He gazed into her eyes for a long moment. "Ye've done right by him, Ina."

"Then lay him to his rest."

"I'll return ye upstairs."

She glanced over her shoulder. "May I remain here in the hall?"

He nodded. "Where would ye—"

"She can sit here, m'laird. She can." Izbeil sat Davina's high-backed chair from the dais near the trestle tables.

"Ye can rest yer leg on this, m'lady." Aleen placed a milking stool in front of the chair, and one of the young lasses put a small pillow on top.

Izbeil led her from Callen's side. "We'll take good care of her, m'laird. That we will."

Callen released her fingers. "Of that, I have no doubts, Izbeil. But if she were to tire before I returned …"

Davina kissed the back of his hand before she let go. "I'll be fine. The earth is soft and the internment should be quick. Ye shan't be long."

Callen watched her move to the chair. "I'll return with all due haste."

The men placed Fergus' body into the coffin, and Callen helped carry it out of the hall. The remaining men filed out behind them. As soon as they were gone, women cleaned the table where the former laird had lain and set the hall to right again.

Izbeil returned to her side and draped her in a plaid. "Do ye require anythin' else, m'lady?"

"Might ye bring me one of Molly's treats?" Davina grinned.

A baby fussed.

"Una." Davina waved her closer. "Come sit with me a spell. Let me see yer wee bairn."

"Would ye care to hold him?"

Davina raised her splinted wrist. "Best not. I don't have a good grasp right now."

They sat and talked before another woman came and took Una's place and then another. Everyone wanted a moment with her. Davina was home.

But her gaze turned toward the door. There was one place she *needed* to go and one she *wanted* to visit.

Chapter 48

Callen couldn't suppress the spring in his step or the smile turning his lips. He led his new kin across the wide expanse, which lay opposite the manse—his manse. With no room within the walls to bury their dead, they'd brought Fergus to the consecrated land where they buried all the inhabitants of the manse. Where one day they would inter he and Ina. His strides lengthened as his chest puffed.

He passed the spot turned by horses' hooves around a patch of grass stained with blood. He couldn't believe only a couple of days had passed since he reunited with his bride. So much had changed.

With the former laird laid to his final rest, Callen turned his gaze back to the powerful walls of Seycoll. The responsibility of over two hundred souls now rested on him. He prayed he was up to such a challenge.

A hand slapped down on his back, jarring him from his thoughts. "Laird Callen."

He couldn't contain his laughter at his friend Neil's roguish grin as the man joined him, leading his horse. "Aye, I'm Laird Callen, as I was a fortnight ago."

"Nay, not the same man at all. Then, ye struggled to win yer lady's heart and find a way to provide for yer comin' bairns. Now, ye're laird of Seycoll, one of the most powerful manses in this part of the highlands."

As they followed the sloping road down to the spit of land connecting Seycoll to the rest of the mainland. Down in the valley the wind remained still. Here on the coast, the air was as restless as it had been in Bottleigh. Yet here, the stirring wind left him calm—even in the face of managing such a powerful holding. He inhaled deep of the salty air. God was good.

"Ye think ye can smile any broader?" Neil laughed.

Callen chuckled. "Not without causin' injury."

Neil's voice sobered. "Speakin' of injuries, how is yer lady?"

"Stubborn. Insisted on comin' down to the wake. Even threatened to manage the stairs on her own if Izbeil or I didn't assist her." Callen sighed. "The ankle and wrist will heal given time, but the headaches and dizziness worry me."

"That too will heal, brother. God hasn't brought the two of ye this far to leave her sufferin'." Neil punched him in the arm. "Ye know, ye must always keep yer lady happy."

"As is true of any husband." He didn't see his friend's point.

"But even more so in Seycoll." Neil lowered his voice. "Ye stir her ire and the entire manse will skin ye."

Callen nodded. "Aye, Fergus warned me in a similar manner. I think it surprised him how they turned on him when he sent her to safety."

"Accordin' to some, Fergus made them believe she'd died after Nathair stabbed her. He only told them the truth to save his own life," Neil said with a hum.

Callen shook his head. In many ways, Fergus was a fool. "I bless Fergus—God rest his soul. But had the man been honest concernin' Davina from the beginnin', He could have avoided much pain."

Neil nodded his agreement as they climbed the road toward the gate.

"Oh, that woman is goin' to be the death of me." Callen groaned as they passed through the gate. Davina had her arm draped over Izbeil's shoulders as they stepped off the last step into the courtyard. Callen quickened his steps. "What are ye doin'?"

She offered him a sheepish grin. "I heard ye returning."

He crossed his arms, and his jaw tightened. "And ye risked further injury to greet me?"

"I missed ye."

Callen fought the smile toying on his lips. "Why does that sound more like a question than an endearment?"

"The lady insisted on goin' to the kirk." Izbeil blurted. "Has it in her 'ead 'tis the only place to pray." Izbeil ducked out from under Davina's arm and passed her to Callen. "As if the Lord Almighty can't hear prayers spoken anywhere. Foolishness, to be sure. Foolishness, I say." She stomped off without a backward glance.

"So, what is so all fired important ye couldn't wait until the Lord's Day two days hence?"

"When I lived here, it was me habit to pray every morn—rain or shine." Her head tucked low to her chest, forcing Callen to place a finger under her chin and raise it again. "I've been neglecting meeting with the Lord."

"Ye've been angry."

Davina sighed as more of her weight rested against his hands at her waist. "I'd like to say sad, not angry. But I fear ye have the right of it."

He scooped her up and cradled her close to his beating heart. "Then, let us both go ask our Lord for forgiveness and give Him praise for how He has provided for us."

She gripped his tunic and closed her eyes as he spun them around. He needed to be more mindful of her dizziness. She swallowed hard before she spoke. "What have ye done that needs forgiving?"

He sighed. "Near refusin' ye hand and missin' out on the deepest love I've ever known."

"And Seycoll."

"Nay, lass." He kissed her forehead as he struggled to unlatch the door while cradling her. A boy ran up and held it open for them.

"Thank ye, Lenox," she said.

"Welcome home, m'lady," the lad beamed, dipping a bow.

Callen carried her toward the altar and sat her on the front pew. "Seycoll is a blessin', to be sure. Somethin' beyond what I ever dreamed for us. But ye, Ina …" He stroked her cheek. "If I lost Seycoll, the title laird, a roof over me head, I trust God to make a way for me—for us. But if I lost ye, would send me straight to the grave, as it did Fergus. I'd live anywhere, do anythin', as long as ye are beside me."

She leaned over and kissed him.

"Is it proper to kiss in the Lord's House?" He chuckled.

Her smile was devilish. "Are we not to greet the brethren with a holy kiss?"

"Sweetness, that is quite a different kind of kiss." He held her gaze as his thumb brushed over the back of her hand.

She flashed him a rather sassy grin and moved as though she might kneel.

"What do ye think ye are doin' now?"

"I suffered no injuries to me knees."

He crossed his arms and raised a brow. "And how do ye propose to rise?"

"I'm counting on a strong, handsome," she moved her lips closer to him with each description as her words grew more breathless, "kind, loving man to offer to pick me up."

The door at the side of the altar creaked open and a brown-robed man with a tonsured head stepped in.

"And there he is now." She tipped her head at the newcomer with a cheeky smirk. What had come over his quiet—almost to the point of being withdrawn—bride? Who was this playful, gorgeous woman teasing him?

"Sister." The monk crossed to her in long strides and gave her a proper holy kiss, with a brief tap of his lips to each freckled cheek. "Oh, the Lord bless ye're return. Sore we've missed ye, lass." His hand extended toward Callen. "And we welcome ye, brother."

"Thank ye." Callen grasped the man's sturdy forearm, his fingers tingled as the monk gripped him as well. This man would be better suited on the back of a warhorse than in monk's robes.

"Glad I am to see ye both to prayers. I'll not disturb ye further, other than to bless ye." The monk's mighty hand landed on his head before Callen bowed it. The man's little finger and thumb brushed the top of each ear. Callen dared a glance at Davina, but the monk was mindful of her injury so his hand only skimmed the crown of her head.

"The Lord's guidin' hand be with ye. May He bless ye with health, strong, God-fearin' bairns, and a long rule of kindness, friendship, and love. Ye bless us, as the Lord covers ye with blessin'."

"Thank ye, Brother Patrick," Davina said.

He inclined his head before striding to the front door on his long legs.

When Callen turned back to his wife, he found she'd worked her way to her knees and sat with head bowed and hands clasped. He slid down next to her and spent some time thanking God for all He'd done for them.

Chapter 49

Callen cradled Ina close. Oh, God was so good.

"Might we go one more place before returning to the hall?"

Callen continued across the yard to the keep. "Ina, this is yer first day out after yer latest injury—"

She stroked his face, her fingers raking through his beard as her pale eyes held him in her pleading gaze. "Will only take a wee mite. Please?"

How could he ever refuse such? The Lord help him, but she'd always get her way if she asked like that. "Where am I to take ye?"

Her features brightened as it appeared she ignored any displeasure in his voice. She pointed. "Just there. Atop the wall."

He climbed the steps to the battlements and lower her so she could stand—as best she could on one foot. She leaned against the wall and looked out over the eastern sea. Rays of light broke through the clouds, stretching down to touch the water and paint the waves in golden light. The wind pulled more strands of her flaming hair free of the loose braid. It whipped about her as if given a life of its own.

Then, the clouds shifted and a ray of light broke free of the others shining on the water. It moved toward Seycoll as the waves crashed below, bringing in the tide. Birds cried out in grating screeches as the ray of light climbed the wall. It splashed over Ina and stopped, encasing her in light and igniting her locks as if actual flame.

Air caught in his lungs. His chest swelled, straining against the seams of his borrowed tunic. Could his heart hold this much love?

"Is something the matter?" Davina's head tipped as she studied him. She held her loose hair at her shoulder.

Callen shook his head, searching for the right words. "Saints have mercy, but ye are a bonny lass. That ye choose to love me—"

Her hand reached for him, freeing her hair to fly about her face. He brushed it aside as he cradled her cheek. "It is because ye love me so that I can love at all. Ye mended me shattered heart." Balanced on one foot, she rose on her toes and captured his lips and he found a hint of summer on them.

She lowered and steadied herself again. "Do ye think ye can be happy here?"

"What man couldn't be happy with ye by his side?"

"But this isn't Bottleigh. There are no mountains, no snow."

He threw his arms in the air as he glanced toward heaven. "Praise the Lord."

Davina giggled. "Then ye like the sea and the wind?"

He wrapped an arm around her. "They suit me, but because they bring ye joy, I shall love them."

Her arms wound around his neck, and she pressed against him. Callen warmed and noted her every curve as she reclaimed his lips.

He released her hair to wrap both arms around her, and she opened her mouth to him. Saints, he loved this woman.

A small shiver raced through her.

Callen pressed his forehead against hers. "Best take ye inside before ye catch a chill. I'll not have ye suffer with a fever again." He cradled her in his arms and she snuggled close.

Callen jerked to a stop before they climbed the stairs to the hall.

She'd been busy thanking God again for such a man to love her, she hadn't noticed someone blocking their path. Davina glanced at the man barring their way. "Matthew, glad I am to see ye well."

"And ye, m'lady."

"Callen, this is Matthew. He served as Fergus' personal guard until they feared what Nathair would do and he became me guard."

Callen sat her on her feet and reached out his hand. "First, I'd thank ye for carin' for Davina so well."

Matthew grasped his arm and nodded. "It was me honor."

"Second, I'd ask if ye be willin' to continue at yer post as her guard. I have a man who's sworn his life to mine, who should be returnin' soon. And while there is little danger to her now within these walls—unless one can die of too much love." He gave her a little squeeze. "There are still those who'd find advantage in capturing the lady of such a powerful holding."

Matthew huffed a deep sigh. "Ye've answered me prayers, m'laird. I'll assure no harm comes to her."

Callen released him and held Davina again. His embrace was both tender and fierce. "I'm trustin' ye with me most cherished treasure, but as I know yer love for her is near as powerful as mine, I'll rest well knowin' ye're on guard."

Matthew bowed and waved out his arm for them to continue. He fell into step behind them.

Cradled back into Callen's arms, she glanced at him. "Do I really need a guard now?"

"Not from those livin' within the walls, as I told Matthew, but when strangers come to call or we venture out."

A thrill burst inside her and made her wiggle. "Venture out?

Where?"

"When ye've have healed well," he said, glancing down at her, "we shall go for a ride in the glen; to the market in Ansmarkt; to visit Bottleigh after our bairns are born."

"Bairns?" Her head dropped to his shoulder as the word whispered out. It warmed every part of her to think of having their children.

He kissed the top of her head. "Aye. As many as God blesses us with."

Heat encased her as they entered the hall with its bright fire, but something more warmed her cheeks.

Callen carried her to the dais and helped her sit before joining her. She laid her hand on his arm. "Ye should speak the grace."

"Oh, right. I'm the laird." He chuckled as he stood and cleared his throat. "I greet ye, me kirth and kin, for what I pray will be many years of cheerful meals together. Shall we bow our heads and give the Lord praise?

"Lord, we thank Ye, for all the wonders of Yer mighty hands. For new family and friends, for returnin' Davina to the kin she loves and who love her. May we never take Yer kindnesses and blessin' for granted and never cease to praise Ye. Bless these who dine here and all who call on Yer name. Amen."

"Amen," everyone answered.

"We are so blessed," she told him as he took his seat.

"Beyond all measure." He served her as Aleen filled her cup. "What's that?"

She lifted the cup to him. "Berry mead. Fergus introduced me to it me first night in Seycoll. I thought they'd run out, but they must have found another barrel. I should save it for special occasions until we can make more."

He shook his head at her offer to try some. "This is why ye taste so sweet. And as this is yer first meal again together with yer people, 'tis a wonderful occasion to celebrate."

As they ate of all her favorite things, she told Callen of each person sitting below. Their names, what work they did in the manse, and their families.

"By the sword, it will take me months to remember everyone."

She shrugged. "I learned them all in a day."

He kissed her temple. "Of course, ye did. Another reason for them to love ye more than me."

She dropped her hands. "They do not."

He kissed her again. "Aye, they do, and I'd have it no other way." He glanced at her plate. "Are ye finished, or would ye like more?"

"I couldn't. As good as it was, I just couldn't find room for another bite."

He wiped his mouth and pushed back his chair. "Then I'll take ye upstairs."

Her hand on his arm kept him from rising. "Might we sit in the solar for a spell?"

He considered her. "Aren't ye tired?"

"Fergus never wanted to share it with me, after Nathair interrupted us with his crude talk the first night. But it is supposed to be a place for the laird and lady to sit and talk and enjoy one another's company."

He smirked as he leaned in close. "Have we not enjoyed one another's company all afternoon, lass?"

"Aye." She let the air ease from her as she gave into him and removed her hand.

He cradled her as she buried her face in his shirt, hoping not to feel the twist of the stairs. She couldn't afford to be queasy on a full stomach. A door creaked open, and he sat her down on a soft chair. There were no cushioned seats in her chamber.

She opened her eyes to the dim solar. Callen lit candles and struck the flint for the fire.

Izbeil poked her head in. "Forgive us, m'lady. We didn't know ye'd be wanting to sit a spell in here."

Davina settled into her chair and brushed her maid's concern off with a sigh. "'Twas a request only a moment ago. There was no way for ye to know."

"If ye have a mind to use the solar often, we'll make sure the fire is struck. We will."

"I would very much favor it." She looked to Callen, who gave his consent.

Izbeil's voice softened and her gaze shifted far off. "Laird Fergus always favored this chamber before Lady Sìle passed. When ye arrived, I thought he would again share the space with ye, but he came to fear yer time together."

"Fear it? Saints above, why?" That made no sense. Nathair had spent little time in the manse to interrupt them.

Izbeil turned to face Davina again. "The laird told me, as ye lay sufferin' from the knife wound, every moment he spent with ye made him love ye more. To the point he feared he wouldn't be able to give ye away when the time came. Yer pleadin' with him as ye did near tore his heart out. He loved ye mightily, m'lady."

Davina stared into the dancing flames of Callen's growing fire. Even their movement made her queasy. "There was so much I didn't ken about what he did. Thank ye for speaking of it, Izbeil."

The maid nodded. "I'll prepare ye chamber for the night." She slipped out before Davina could thank her again.

Callen moved toward her on slow steps, placed his hands on the arms of her chair, and leaned down to hover above her lips. "Now that we are alone in our solar, m'lady, what do ye wish to discuss?"

She nibbled on her lip for a moment.

Callen leaned forward, his arms bending, his gaze searching her face. "What is it?"

She gazed for another moment. "Will ye tell me of yer ponies?"

He smiled, scooped her from her chair, and sat with her in his lap. "I would speak to ye until the sunrise of our fine Highland stock. What would ye like to know?"

She nestled against him with her head on his shoulder. "Everything."

He kissed her head and settled back into the chair.

She listened about his other great love.

Callen moved, tightening his grip on her. Her head popped up, almost colliding with his. "Yer going to stop in the middle? How did ye go from one mare to—how many stallions?"

He chuckled. "I thought yer were asleep."

"Nay, I was listening."

He stood anyway. "'Tis late and ye're still healin'. We will have many evenin's to talk of horses."

"Ye promise?" Her hope had returned, for she already knew her husband would agree.

He glanced at her as they moved toward the doors. "Why do they interest ye so?"

"Ye love them and I want to love them too. Will ye teach me to ride?"

Callen stopped in the middle of the hall between the solar and her chamber. "Ye don't know how to ride?"

"Only been on a horse four times." She brought up a finger as she counted each off. "One: Behind Crom coming here. Two: A ride with Fergus, but someone shot me mount in the flank with an arrow. Three: Carried to yer home. And four; sprawled across Nathair's lap."

"Don't speak of him again." His words were harsh, and she startled. Callen sighed and pressed his forehead to her temple. "I still suffer nightmares of him takin' ye away and all the thin's I feared he'd do to ye, love. The beast is dead. Let him rot and never be remembered."

She cradled his cheek. "I love ye, Callen of the Kincaid, Laird of Seycoll." Her kiss captured his lips, and she savored the taste of him.

"And I ye, Ina. I'd love nothin' more than to teach ye to ride. *When* yer well healed and can sit the saddle without headache or dizziness."

She groaned. "I am always waiting."

He laughed and kissed her cheek. "But the day will come." He took her into her chamber and left her in Izbeil's care. "Rest well, love."

She clung to his fingers and made him pull from her as he entered his chamber from their shared door.

"'Tis good to see ye so happy, m'lady. It is," Izbeil said as she unwound her dress' laces.

Davina threw her arms around her maid's neck and hugged her tight. "Oh, Izbeil, I didn't know a person could be this happy."

Izbeil sputtered and reached to release Davina's grasp. "Saints, lass. Ye're the lady of the manse. Ladies don't go around huggin' the maid. They don't. Isn't proper, I say."

Davina kissed her cheek. "But I love ye, Iz. I missed ye and I'm glad to be under yer care again."

Izbeil stilled and returned the hug. "Ah, lass, we missed ye all the more. I don't know what we would have done if ye hadn't returned."

Chapter 50

"Good morn, m'lady." Quinn bowed as Callen carried her into the hall the next morning. "M'laird."

"Good morn, Quinn." Davina smiled as Callen stood her on her feet and she clung to his arm around her waist and prayed for the dizziness to flee.

The tanner offered her a tall stick with a bowed bit wrapped in leather at the top. "We've made this for ye."

She stared at it, unsure of what to do with the item. "Thank ye." She reached out for it.

Quinn tucked it under his arm and leaned on it while raising one foot. "'Tis a walking stick to help ye move about the hall and yer chamber."

"Oh, that's brilliant."

"Have ye seen no one with an injured leg use one of these?" Callen asked in her ear.

She shook her head and regretted it before she took the walking aid and tried to put it under her arm. But even on the tips of her toes, she couldn't manage it.

Quinn took it again. "Now, don't ye fret, m'lady. It just needs to be shortened a wee bit." He had her stand straight with her arms at her side to judge the needed height. Stepping away, Duncan handed him a small saw and Quinn cut away some of the length. She tried it again and Quinn cut off a bit more before it was easy for her to use.

Horses whinnied in the courtyard. "Sounds like the herd is here," Callen said.

"Ye go check on them. I'll be quite fine with me new walking stick." She took a few slow steps in the space near the dais' stairs.

Callen kissed her temple. "Don't ye go replacin' me so quick, love." He nodded to Matthew as he passed and threw open the hall doors.

Matthew moved closer. "Mind where ye go, m'lady, and don't ye rush. And under no circumstances are ye to traverse stairs with that thin'. We don't want ye injured further."

Ignoring the worried furrow of Matthew's brow, she started moving toward the kitchen. "Thank ye, Quinn and Duncan," she called over her shoulder as she pushed through the door.

"Well, if ye aren't a sight." Molly turned and perched her fists on her hips.

"Hello to ye too, Molly." Davina leaned against the worktable not far inside the door. She was already tired. She scanned the faces working to prepare the morning meal. Aleen had served her mead last eve. They smiled at one another.

Tara stirred a pot and dipped a curtsy. "Welcome home, m'lady."

"Thank ye."

Rachel stepped out of the larder with a sack of apples.

"Rachel! Yer home too?" Davina reached out for her and the maid welcomed her hug.

"As soon as Angus knew *he* was dead, he came and fetched me. Asked for me hand too," Rachel said with a wide smile.

Davina squeezed her hand. "Oh, what a blessing. When do ye speak the consents?"

Rachel's smile grew. "As soon as m'lady can dance the reels with us."

"M'lady, if ye don't require our assistance, I need me lasses to return to their duties so the meal can begin on time." Molly continued to stand akimbo and keep her stern tone, but tears glistened in her eyes.

Davina hobbled to her and spoke in hushed whispers. "I missed ye too, Molly."

The gruff cook couldn't contain her tears. She used the hem of her apron to swipe them away. "Oh, now look what ye've gone and done. Ye've made me a blubberin' mess and I've work to do."

Davina wrapped the arm that wasn't using the walking stick around the cook's shoulders and kissed Molly's head as Callen so often did to her. "Yer work is always the finest, and yer nay a mess."

Molly gave her a tight hug. "Thank ye, m'lady. Ye don't know what yer return means to all of us. Don't know what we'd do without ye here." As if coming to herself again, Molly released her, brushed away her tears and straightened her apron. "I must return to me work." She looked to the other serving maids who stood stone-straight, mouths hanging open. "Oh," Molly huffed with a wave of her hand. "Back to work with the lot of ye. And if ye ever say a word—"

The maids gave a vehement shake of their heads as they resumed their tasks.

"Ye either, m'lady. Love ye as I do, I'll still not take kindly to ye tellin' neither."

Davina's laughter joined with Callen as they each re-entered the hall from opposite sides. A wind-blown, dark-haired man walked beside him and Neil. She knew him to be Callen's guard, but she couldn't recall his name.

They crossed the room to her, but Callen spoke to her guard trailing behind her. "Matthew, this is the man I spoke to ye about. Thomas, this is Matthew, Lady Davina's guard. Matthew, would ye show Thomas around after the meal and get him acquainted with the strengths and weaknesses of Seycoll?"

"Aye, m'laird." Matthew waved out a hand, directing Thomas to a nearby table.

Callen scooped her up and carried her up the dais. Before setting her down, he kissed her cheek. "I may join them so I can get a better understandin' of our holdin's. Can ye spare me this morn?"

"As the gifted walking stick and a visit to the kitchens delayed me visit to the kirk, I shall have enough to keep me occupied."

"Yer not to try the stairs on yer own."

She rolled her eyes and stifled a groan. "Aye, Matthew has already informed me."

Callen's head bobbed once, before he sat her down and said grace.

When she emerged from the kirk later, several of the men were saddling horses outside the stable. She inched her way toward the commotion to see what was happening. Callen saw her and strolled to her.

"Mmm—Margaret? No Maud? The cook."

"Molly."

"Aye, right. Molly has informed me the meat is runnin' low in the larder. We are goin' to see what we might scare up before supper." He kissed her forehead. "Matthew is to stay with ye and I've given him permission to carry ye on the stairs." He strolled away with a swagger she'd not noticed before. He swung up into the saddle, offered her a quick wave, and led the hunting party, which comprised three of his own men and several from Seycoll, out of the gate.

"Do ye wish to return to the hall, m'lady?"

"Nay." She grinned at Matthew. "I wish to be atop the walls and watch them head into the hunting grounds"

Matthew inclined his head. "As ye wish."

Once atop the gate, she watched until she couldn't see them anymore. Then, she hobbled along the battlements to the seaside and watched the waves beat against the rocks and corncrake, gull, and gannet whirl on the currents of air.

"M'lady!"

She turned to look into the courtyard. Quinn's eldest, Nathan, stood next to a man she didn't know. His plaid was neat and his dress formal.

"Ye have a visitor, m'lady," Nathan shouted.

She nodded to Nathan, and Matthew carried her down the stairs. He stood close to her as the man bowed and introduced himself.

"Good day to ye, Lady Davina. I am Jock, the king's page."

Davina's heart leapt, and she tried to swallow.

"The king bids you greeting and will be here to visit Seycoll this eve."

Oh, saints above, they entertained the king this night with only hours to prepare and—

Her heart beat so fast she feared she might faint. Had he consented to Fergus' request? Oh, please! He could not come to take Seycoll away from them.

She forced her words out with a calm assurance she didn't feel. "Of course, Jock, Seycoll will be most honored to welcome our great king." Using her walking stick, she moved toward the hall.

Jock fell into step beside her. "Are ye injured, m'lady?"

Saints! If she said yes, would he tell the king she was too weak to oversee the manse? While it was clear she needed help walking now, Luke had assured her it wouldn't always be so.

"Nathair, Laird Fergus' son, inflicted serious injuries on our lady when he kidnapped her from Bottleigh," Matthew said.

Jock inclined his head. "I give thanks to the Almighty you are on the mend, my lady."

"Thank ye. Might ye tell me some of the king's preferences for his meals? I may not have everything on hand, but—"

Jock raised his hand as they approached the stairs. "There is no need to trouble yourselves. The king is just passing this way and hoped to have a word with Laird Fullarton, but I have learned of his passing. I'm sure he will want to meet with you and your husband before resuming the trail."

"If the king comes to Seycoll, we shall show him the honor he is due." Davina was firm, though every part of her quaked at the thought of what words her king would share with her.

"I will inform the king of your welcome." Jock bowed and returned to his waiting horse.

"Matthew, take me to Molly. Quick."

Chapter 51

"Ina, whatever is the matter?" Callen caught her as she loped past him without acknowledging his return.

"The king comes to visit—this night." She turned to Izbeil, who hurried past her in the other direction. "Is the laird's chamber ready?"

Izbeil never slowed. "Almost. Will be done long before the king shows his face. It will."

Davina had turned her attention back to him, as he still held her in place. "Did Izbeil sound angry?"

"What is happening to me chamber?" Callen glanced at the harried movements of all those around him.

Her features pinched as though she thought him daft. "We prepare it for the king's visit."

He smirked at her. "And where am I to sleep?"

"Ye mean if the king allows us to remain?" She shuddered in his grasp. "Did Fergus say if the king ever gave his consent to giving Seycoll to me?"

"Nay, lass." He rubbed her arm. "Just that he sent word to the king of his intentions. But our king thought well of Fergus. Try not to fret."

"But he could take it all—"

He kissed her silent. "Trust that all will be well."

"But—"

Stopped her words with a kiss again. "Trust. And ye never said where I was to sleep if the king has me bed."

Her head cocked. "With me. Where else would ye lay?"

Oh, if she only knew what she did to him. He may have to sleep in a chamber on the second floor. She remained too injured for him to share her bed.

Davina tried to pull from his hold. "The rooms on the second floor are being readied for his officials. But Matthew thinks he'll be traveling with many. How do we house and feed them all?"

"We brought down three stag and two large boars. There will be meat for all. I best see the pits are dug and the fires begun. There is little time before they arrive." He offered her a tight hugged and assured her with another kiss. "All will be well. We shall show our king our loyalty and he shall continue on his way, leavin' us as we are." But even he worried over what word the king may bring them. *Lord, please let him bring good news.*

Davina hobbled beside him. "I'll go to the kirk and pray."

Callen shook his head. "I need Matthew with me. Ye see to the preparin' of the hall and the keep."

They went in opposite directions. Ina shuffling, and Callen at a near run. So much needed to be done and so little time remained.

The hall filled with the inhabitants of Seycoll. Those she loved. Did the buzz of their conversation sound angry? She imagined the worst. She focused on their preparations she couldn't help with. The rooms were prepared. Meat was roasting. A fire built high. The hall swept clean, and fresh reeds laid and sprinkled with sweet herbs. She drew in a deep breath of their fragrance in hopes it would calm her nerves. It didn't.

She sat on the end of a bench at one of the common tables. The maids laid the table atop the dais for the king. She'd pace if she didn't already ache from all the hobbling she'd done with her stick throughout the day. She needed Callen to tell her again all would be well. But he waited outside to greet the king when he arrived. She'd wanted to join him, but Callen convinced her it would not make a good impression to be carried about.

How long would they have to wait? Her fingers drummed on the tabletop. Her people milled around as if they were as restless as she.

How much longer?

The main doors pushed open, making everyone jump. Davina rose and watched as King Robert II strolled in with a bright smile. Many of his men trailed him and Callen followed with Thomas, Neil, Owen, and Duncan. Callen and the men of Seycoll came to stand around her. The king continued on to the dais as his men took a place at another table with the people of Seycoll.

King Robert was about the same height as Callen, though much older. He wore his gray hair over his ears and bore a long beard and mustache. The king stood behind the high table. Callen took a knee and Davina attempted to curtsy. Unfortunately, between the dizziness and the splint, she lost her balance. Callen captured her around the waist and brought her to sit on his upturned knee. It wasn't a proper observance, but at least she hadn't ended up sprawled on the floor in front of the king.

As she caught her breath, she realized that most of her people still stood. Oh, by all the saints above, what were they doing? Didn't they understand how important it was that they all appear as loyal subjects?

Davina dared a glance at the king. "Yer majesty, I beg yer forgiveness —"

The king raised his hand, cutting off her plea, and her heart dropped into the pit of her already queasy stomach. "No need, my lady. I see the loyalty and the heart of a people who don't know if they might trust the man who now stands before them. Let me start by assuring all that I do not come to act against Laird Fergus' wishes. Lady Davina is the legitimate heir to Seycoll and the man she has wed, Laird Callen."

At those words, every knee touched the floor, and they uttered the first words of the oath as they had done for her.

Again, the king's hand rose. "I thank you, but there is no need for such formalities. Laird Callen gave his oath when I entered the gate and, as it is clear you all follow your lady, I trust you at your laird's word to remain faithful Scotts.

"Now, Laird Callen, if you would bring your bonny lady up, might I be so bold as to request we begin the meal? Something smells wondrous and me men and I are famished."

Before she could protest, Callen carried her to the high table where men added their chairs beside the king's. Callen settled her and gave the grace, praising God and thanking the king.

Before he sat on Davina's right, the king grasped Callen's forearm, "Good it is to see you again, Callen. How is your Da?"

"Well, Yer Majesty. And Dougal, does he still ride with ye?"

The king shook his head. "Departed for Bottleigh not a fortnight ago. Let us sit and eat and I shall tell you the tale. But may I caution you, friend?" He glanced out over those dining with them. "Be mindful of how you treat your bonny lass. I think they'll turn on you if you displease her."

"Aye," Callen chuckled. "Ye're the third man to warn me of such."

The men sat on either side of her as the maids brought trays of food to the tables. "We expected Dougal afore the winter set in," Callen began as he filled her plate.

Saints, she was tired and her husband was not attending to what he was doing. He heaped her plate with twice the normal quantity she ate.

She stared at the mound and sighed. Had she too good ankles, she'd excuse herself and retire to her chambers. But she didn't, and this was not any night in Seycoll. The king himself sat beside her.

King Robert drew his dinner knife and a flash of candle light on its blade took Davina to the night Nathair stabbed her. King Robert's words soon brought her back to the present. "I encouraged your brother more than once to return; he seemed reluctant. As we wintered in Aberdour, I spoke to him more than once. He'd always say you were there to help your father, and I had greater need of him on the battlefield than what he could provide at home." The king chewed a bit of boar and hummed his pleasure.

King Robert smiled and continued. "I called Dougal to me a couple weeks ago when the weather was the worst after I received news of your marriage to this bonny lass." The king saluted her with his fork. "It wasn't until I told him your marriage made you the laird of Seycoll that he was eager to return home."

Callen ate nothing as he listened with rapt attention. "Why would it matter if I was laird or not?"

The king considered his words before speaking. "I think he didn't want you to feel put upon by his presence." The king captured Davina's attention again; she'd taken only a few bites of her food. "'Tis wonderful to be greeted with such graciousness and served such a fine meal. And to include all me retainers and attendants is beyond the call of hospitality, my lady. I can see some of the many reasons Fergus favored you so."

"Thank ye, Yer Majesty. Molly is a wonder in the kitchens and the maids worked very hard. I shall tell them all their labors were appreciated."

"And that is why yer kin love ye so." Raising his gaze, he smiled at Callen again. "You are a mighty lucky man, Kincaid!"

Callen rested his hand on her back. "Nay, Majesty. I am blessed beyond all comprehension."

The king raised his cup to the two of them. "To God's blessings."

The men's conversation turned to the struggles with the Scottish lairds and the constant threat from England. Davina fought to lift the next bite to her lips and chew without falling asleep face first on her plate.

"Callen, my friend, I think it high time you take your bonny lass to her chambers."

Davina's head jerked up. "Yer Majesty, forgive me …"

"You've naught to apologize for, my lady. I know you still suffer from your recent injuries, and you've worked hard to welcome me on far too short a notice. Please, take your rest. Perhaps you and your laird will visit me in Stirling this summer."

"Thank ye for yer kindness, Majesty." Davina stifled a yawn.

King Robert nodded to her and to Callen as he scooped her up in his arm.

"The laird's chamber is prepared for ye, Sire," she said around another yawn. He replied, but she didn't hear his words. Saints, she was tired.

Chapter 52

Davina woke with the first cries of the many sea birds outside. She stretched her stiff muscles and reached across the empty bed. A quick scan revealed Callen hadn't joined her. Her bedcoverings hadn't been disturbed and—was she still wearing yesterday's gown? She sat up, threw off the covers, and opened the curtain around her bed.

"Ah, she wakes." Izbeil bustled about the room. "The laird said ye were asleep in his arms before he touched the first step. Ye were so shattered, I couldn't bring meself to wake ye to undress. We thought ye might sleep through the day. We did."

"Where is the laird?"

Izbeil turned to straighten the bed. "He's off biddin' the king farewell."

Davina glanced toward the windows where the shutters were only open a crack. Was the sun anywhere near rising? She inched toward the edge of the bed and sat still, waiting for the dizziness the movement stirred to flee. She prayed again that it would just be gone forever.

"Why don't ye rest for a spell longer, m'lady?"

"I'd like to go to prayers. I have much to be grateful for."

Izbeil narrowed her gaze and sighed, but didn't say more than, "Matthew awaits."

As Matthew carried her into the great hall, a commotion caught their attention. A few of her kin were at the boards for the morning meal, but the shouts from outside caused Matthew to alter his course from taking her to the kirk to carrying her up on the dais instead. He retreated down the stairs and stood with his hand on his hilt.

The rumble outside grew.

Davina stood behind her chair and gripped the back to steady herself.

The unintelligible noise turned into a guttural shout as the doors burst open. "Davina!"

Oh, saints above, aid her. Crom shook off several hands as they attempted to seize him and halt his progress. "DAVINA!"

"By the saints, Crom, I stand here," Davina said as her knuckles turned white against the dark wood of the chair.

Callen followed in Crom's wake with several others. "What do ye be wanting with the lady?" He stepped in front of the high table between her and her da.

Crom marched toward him with a growl. "I speak to Davina and it be none of yer concern."

Callen took a wide stance and crossed his arms. "As I'm her husband, I can assure you it *is* of my greatest concern."

Crom's gaze narrowed on her. "What? Did ye go and kill another one? Fie, child, ye are tough on a man."

Davina swallowed her embarrassment as she confronted Crom. "Fergus was never me husband. And in his last breaths, he saved me life."

Crom balled up his fist. "I had a contract with that old buzzard. He was to marry ye when I sold ye to him."

Strength flood her being and she narrowed her gaze. "The contract ye signed made me his ward. And *he* attended his duties *well.*"

Crom ignored the chastisement of her upbringing. He pointed a finger at her. "Ye need to give me money, Davina. Ye owe me for making such a fine match for ye." His wagging finger swung toward Callen while his lip curled in a sneer. "Fergus spoke against me so I've lost most me business."

"The lady owes you naught. And a fine Scottish citizen such as Lady Davina is never to be sold." The voice came from behind Crom, where many had gathered to see what was happening before the morning meal was served. The voice was deep. She knew it, but couldn't place it straight away.

"Stay out of this, peasant!" Crom barked

Then, her gaze landed on four hooded men seated at the center table. Saints, alive! She gripped the chairs and bent in observance. "Yer Majesty."

"Majesty?" Crom spun as the men stood, revealing themselves as King Robert and his guards.

The king glanced up at her. "Lady Davina, we will take this vermin with us and deposit him in the first quarry we happen past. He'll not bother ye again." King Robert motioned to his guards, who stepped forward to secure Crom.

Crom whirled and lunged toward the dais. "Davina, help me, child."

Matthew held him a few steps away at the point of his sword. Davina hobbled around the high table without her walking stick and Callen lifted her to the floor. Leaning on him, she hobbled toward Crom.

"I fear, Crom, there is naught that I can do, being a useless woman and all." He glared as she threw his words from her childhood back at him. "I tried all me days under yer roof, Crom, to be obedient, respectful, and do all ye asked in hopes of even one kind word. But I received none from ye. I did not protest or fight when you sold me to Ealar nor to Fergus. But even in this I could do naught to earn yer kindness.

"Now, the high king of Scotland, my liege laird, has spoken and I'll not go against him. Ye have set yer path, now ye must walk it." Davina stepped toward him and brushed his cheek, but he jerked from her touch. "I forgive ye, though. For what ye meant for me harm, God has used to bless me beyond all measure. May God in turn show ye mercy wherever He is sending ye."

"Ye filthy wretch!"

Before Crom could lunge at her, the king slugged him in the jaw and sent him reeling back several steps. "Mind yerself, man." The wave of the king's arm took in those around them. "These good folk will tear ye limb from limb if ye so much as say another cruel word to their beloved lady."

Crom did glance at all the angry faces and the feasting knives, dirks, and swords ready to run him through. He spit on the ground at her feet and muttered a curse no one could hear. His hands were bound, the guards led he out, and her kin followed, brandishing their weapons at him.

Callen hugged her tight.

Callen provided a horse from Fergus' stables for Crom to ride so he wouldn't slow the king much. When King Robert and all he's retainers were out the gate, he turned and headed back into the hall and Davina.

A movement caught his eye as he crossed the courtyard. She stood atop the battlements in her favorite corner. He climbed to join her and slipped his arms around her waist. She leaned back into him and they stared out over the quiet sea. The sun set on the horizon and painted the water in shades of yellow and gold. Birds whirled to the sea, dove below the surface, emerged with fish in their beaks, and returned to their nests. The gentle lapping of the waves washed away the tension of the last day.

Davina's hands covered his and laced their fingers together. Her head rested under his chin and she released a long, slow breath.

"All is well, me love. Ye have the king's favor and yer beloved Seycoll. Crom will never darken our door again. What more can I do for ye?"

She turned and wrapped her arms around his neck, careful not to scratch him with her splint.

With tenderness, he worked his fingers through her braid, releasing her hair to float on the gentle breeze.

She gazed into his eyes with such love it near stopped his heart. "Give me bairns."

He captured her lips, savoring her sweetness, and scooped her into his arms.

Glossary

Arisaid – Scottish women's garment where a long strip of plaid is wrapped over the head and down the shoulders past the waist.

Blighter – a person regarded with contempt, irritation, or pity

Breeks – trousers

Burghers – a citizen of a borough or town, especially one belonging to the middle class.

Cabinet – a room used as a study or office or just a sitting room.

Camen – the stick in stinty game.

Chamberlain – took care of the personal well-being of the lord and his family

Dirk – a dagger, especially of the Scottish Highlands.

Garron Pony – In Scotland, a garron is one of the types of Highland pony. It is the larger, heavier type bred on the mainland.

Kirk – Scottish church

Kirth and Kin – Scottish friends and family

Laird – Scottish lord

Life-cycle service – training for both male and female leaving home to become domestic and agricultural servants and marrying afterwards in their twenties

Manse – the dwelling of a landholder; mansion in the thirteenth century

Marshal – oversaw military, arms and discipline, knights, squires, men at arms

Night rail - nightgown

Score – an old word for the number twenty

Sennight – one week

Shinty – Scottish game resembling field hockey

Solar – a sort of early drawing room

Steward – a person who manages another's property or financial affairs; one who administers anything as the agent of another or others.

Tonsure – a haircut common of some monks where the crown of the head is shaved bald and the sides and bangs allowed to grow a few inches long

Trestle Table – is an item of furniture consisting of two or three trestle supports linked by a longitudinal cross-member over which a board or tabletop is placed.

Trews – close-fitting tartan trousers

Waesucks – from Scots Middle English "woe's sakes."

About the Author

Michelle Janene (Murray) is a teacher by day and writes Christian fantasy and historical fiction in all her free time. She lives in Northern California with two crazy dogs and the characters of her imagination.

If you enjoyed *Lost Stones: A Savior Stone Chronicle* please review it on your favorite site.

Join Michelle's email list and get a free novelette at
MichelleJanene.com
You can also connect with Michelle:
Facebook: Michelle Janene-Author or Strong Tower Press
Twitter: @MichelleJaneneM
Instagram: michellejanene_author
Pinterest: www.pinterest.com/michellejanene
Goodreads: Michelle Janene
StrongTowerPress.com

Other Books

Check out these books also by Michelle

Mission: Mistaken Identity

The Changed Heart Series:
God's Rebel
Rebel's Son
Hidden Rebel

Seer of Windmere

Barbarian Hero

Guardians of Truth

Culling a Miracle

Lost Stones

The Last Good King

The King's Vengeance